MARGIN NOTES

Tom -
yes, it's my
book; yes, I
book; wrote it and
yes, you're
in the river...

Catherine Walker-Gilman

iUniverse, Inc.
New York   Bloomington

Margin Notes

iUniverse books may be ordered through booksellers or by contacting:

iUniverse
1663 Liberty Drive
Bloomington, IN 47403
www.iuniverse.com
1-800-Authors (1-800-288-4677)

ISBN: 978-1-4401-4017-4 (sc)
ISBN: 978-1-4401-4018-1 (e-book)

Printed in the United States of America

iUniverse rev. date: 5/1/2009

For my beloved Jason, Rowan, and Quinn for encouraging me to be so many different people all at once…

Generations do not cease to be born, and we are responsible to them because we are the only witnesses they have. The sea rises, the light fails, lovers cling to each other, and children cling to us. The moment we cease to hold each other, the sea engulfs us and the light goes out.

— *James Baldwin*

Contents

vii

MISSION IMPROBABLE

I am sitting in the middle of a juniper bush bargaining with a gigantic, wooly monster. This juniper bush may appear harmless at first glance, but its needles are impaling me with even the slightest change in position. And the foliage gives off a distinctive odor, somewhere between cat pee and skunk. Every time I shift to wake up my sleeping feet, the smell seems to get stronger. I know it's permeating my clothes. I imagine it will never leave. How am I supposed to attract the attention of my one true love in a positive way if I smell like a litter box?

I am Byron Jones. My one true love is Lily Tinker. And the wooly monster is a gargantuan English sheepdog. I am in an awkward position to say the least, and I am not sure how to proceed. I need an Aston Martin, or maybe a jet pack like Sean Connery in *Thunderball*. That would be just the ticket.

How did I end up in the shrubbery? You might well ask. It is a long and complicated story, and to understand it, you really need to know a little bit more about who I am.

I have some time to kill. The wooly sentinel doesn't appear to be going anywhere any time soon. He's not barking, or even growling. He just has me cornered and is creating a substantial pool of drool that is dripping directly onto my left shoe. If anything, he seems to want to bond. But that is not my mission. I am a patient boy, though. While I wait for my captor to get bored and go inside, I'll fill you in on my story so far. My life is one big cliché in a lot of ways, so I may as well

1

start with one. I guess I'll begin at the beginning. But that means I need to figure out where the beginning is…it goes something like this.

I was born in Roswell, New Mexico. This is a town where space aliens supposedly landed not so long ago, and where the government has theoretically created this great cover-up story and fooled the American public about not being alone in the universe. It is merely a coincidence that I was born there. I am not an alien, although I have been accused of alien-type behavior on more than one occasion. My mom and my natural dad, as it happens, were obsessed with UFOs. They moved to Roswell expressly to keep an eye on things, in the hopes of having a close encounter. My only memories of Roswell are pretty vague: a yellow and white afghan supposedly knitted by my Grandma, howling sand storms, and predatory cacti in the "field" behind the trailer, the smells of lightning and o-zone. I asked my mom about all these things years later, and she didn't believe that I remembered any of it. Little did she know I was a child prodigy with a razor-sharp memory. My mind is a font of useless information. That's one of my most endearing personality traits. I can remind family and friends of exceptionally stupid things they've said five years in the past at awkward moments. It's a natural talent.

Anyhow, whether my parents ever actually communed with an extra terrestrial I couldn't say. They split up when I was still in diapers, and my mom and I moved on. I don't really recall my dad at all, except for a vague, stooped shadow with a slightly acidic smell, sort of vinegary and citrusy, following it around. I guess they had "irreconcilable differences," namely, my mom didn't care for having household items flung at her head on a regular basis. So my mom and I spent the next few years touring around the vast, undefined middle of the United States in a Winnebago. I learned to drive the thing when I was nine, yes, a terrifying prospect, but I am a tall kid. I was able to reach the pedals at an early age. On more than one occasion my mom was pulled over on a rural highway in Wyoming or Kansas as I scrambled into the passenger seat.

Confounded dog! Stop breathing on me!

It wasn't necessarily a *bad* life; it was just a *bizarre* one. We focused our pit stops on locations known for extra-terrestrial sightings or suspicious craters, things like that. Most kids have their pictures taken in the fall at school in front of a cheesy backdrop of apple trees and fake fallen leaves. Me, I had my picture taken in front of potentially supernatural American landmarks. For example, there is currently an 8x10 glossy of me in an atrocious metallic golden frame sitting on our TV. I am standing in front of Devil's Tower in Wyoming. This is a remarkably shaped mountain. It is almost vertical, and looks kind of like a gigantic chimney or a top hat. But this aspect of the monument does not interest my mom one little bit. She took my picture there because of a movie, a movie that speaks the *truth*, she says.

You see, Devil's Tower is the infamous mountain from the classic 1977 film *Close Encounters of the Third Kind*. I am so not joking. It's bad enough that my mom insists on posing me in front of alien hotspots, but this one isn't even bordering on reality. It's from a Hollywood blockbuster for crying out loud! So there I stand. I am not looking at the camera. Instead, my mom told me to gaze slightly upward and off into the distance as though psychically summoning a gangly, googly-eyed visitor. This is typical of my life so far. My mother is a freak.

This is how we lived for a lot of years. I spent a few months, at best, in any one school before my mom would wake up one morning and decide that the "cosmic energy" wasn't right. So we would pack up and go at the drop of a hat. It's hard to make friends under these circumstances, even harder to actually learn anything at school. Fortunately, I'm a good reader, so I have taught myself a vast amount of information about a wide variety of topics. There was always a pile of overdue library books belonging to libraries from Brooklyn to Seattle scattered about the Winnebago. Librarians are suckers for kids who show an interest in being functionally literate.

I think I saw a seagull over there. What on earth is a seagull doing loitering in this neck of the woods? Does it not know that we're landlocked?

But I didn't really enjoy living that way. Needless to say, I was pretty relieved when Mom hooked up with Diesel. That is, disturbingly, his legal name. I asked him last week, purely to tick him off, if he had a brother named ethanol. He didn't understand the question, but he got that it was not a compliment and ran me out of the garage with a plunger, the nearest available weapon.

Diesel's not all bad; he's just not the sharpest tool in the shed.

He sees himself as the ultimate Harley guy. What he actually is is a Weekend Warrior. Every Sunday afternoon, rain or shine, he follows the same routine. He sheds his preppy Polo shirt and his Dockers and transforms himself into Mad Max. I am talking black leather pants cinched too tightly around his middle-aged spread, a matching black leather vest, a black button-down shirt, and a totally decked out biker jacket. He looks like a complete moron, but neither my mom nor I have the heart to tell him. He is almost as devoted to his $30,000 hog as he is to my mother. Almost. And that's the reason I tolerate him. That's the reason I let him stick around. There are days when he comes home with bunches of faded flowers from the grocery store, or those goofy cards that play music. In his own dorky way, I think he really cares about her.

Still, it'd be easy enough to get rid of Diesel if I so desired. I have accomplished this feat with numerous would-be-boyfriends of my mother's in years past. But it seems like Mom really cares about Diesel, enough to settle down and buy a house. Enough to apply for a job without announcing to the potential employer that there's a space alien answering the phone at the front desk. By golly, she deserves a little happiness. And I'm hoping that living with someone who doesn't navigate life like a character in an H.G. Wells novel might do her some good. Mom grumbles a little about her oh-so-mundane receptionist's job, but she tempers the boredom with attendance of annual Star-Cons in and around Colorado. Her persona of choice is trashy Vulcan drag queen, or something along those lines, accompanied by Diesel in his dubiously relevant leather chaps. Whatever floats your boat, I say. We haven't moved in three years, and I'm good with that. I'm feeling old and jaded for my twelve years.

I am trying to do that trick right now where you pat your head and rub your tummy at the same time. It truly is a mystery, isn't it? I love natural anomalies.

So I am relatively happy living here in Asheville. It's a pretty small hamlet a few miles off the highway, plopped in between Denver and Boulder. Asheville is an old mining town. A lot of ancient folks live here too, but as they die off, lots of families with kids are moving into their quaint little houses. Last month my ferret, Carmen, disappeared through the boards covering an old mine shaft in the woods behind our house. I thought she was a goner, but she emerged from the linen closet in our house a week later. Makes you wonder, doesn't it?

So this is an all right little place. It's kind of sleepy. Not a lot happens here. I attend Asheville Middle, and by most accounts, it would be great if I went somewhere else. I like school ok, but school doesn't think a whole lot of me. I have a label you see. I am…drum roll please…"Twice Exceptional." Not once, but twice. My teachers and the principal at A.M.S will tell you that loosely translated this label means "Pain in the Behind." Whatever. I am who I am. I didn't choose my genes.

This is how I believe my teachers and Mr. Otto, the principal, see me. I trudge through the door with my head down. I am usually wearing a Rockies cap, so I have to be reminded, loudly to remove it. You see, everyone assumes I am an intentional troublemaker, that I'm trying to push the buttons of every adult in the building. Although I'd like to take credit for being aware of my ability to irk people, I honestly don't usually know I'm doing it. The hat, for example, is kind of a part of my personality. I always wear it, even when I go to bed. It's kind of like a security blanket. I also like to think it keeps the variety of voices in my head from slipping out, but that's another story. Pathetic, yes? Anyway, when I walk in that door at 7:30 Mr. Otto is usually the first one to see me, and the first one to holler at me for insubordination. I can hear him right now muttering a few curses under his breath punctuated with "defiant delinquent" and "disgusting headgear." You get the picture.

So after I remove the hat, I head for my locker. I catch numerous glimpses from teachers on hall duty, and lots of the kids whisper about me behind their not-very-secretive hands. I do have a tendency to mutter to myself as I walk down the halls, and I rarely initiate human contact. I don't mean to be rude, but part of this whole "exceptional" business seems to be that I have a lot going on in my head. In fact, it's a little like the commentary for a really random documentary. My brain hops from subject to subject constantly, and rarely turns off. So sometimes I have conversations with my brain. That's all I'm doing when I'm talking to myself. I don't really care if anyone "gets it" or not. I need to talk through what I'm thinking in order to go on with my day. If that makes me a psycho, so be it. When Marcus Beech made a snide comment about my muttering the other day I informed him that I was channeling Martians through my braces. That did the trick. He flipped me the bird and galumphed off down the hall in his classy neanderthalish swagger.

Who were the Neanderthals anyways? Why do they get such a bad rap? Maybe I'm being unfair by taking their name in vain. Good thing they aren't around to beat me with a club or something.

So that's one half of my exceptionality. I am super-smart. You know, IQ off the charts, "Oh my goodness Ms. Jones, he's a genius!" That kind of thing. I read all the time, and I remember pretty much every word. But then I can also take the ideas I've read and manipulate them. I like to think about "what if?" kinds of issues. I think this definitely freaks my teachers out. You know, things like, "What if what Orwell really meant was that we should raise animals to an equal level with us?" or "What if we are actually living in a parallel universe, and our evil twins are watching us from afar?" I'm certainly not claiming that my ideas are *correct*, I just like to think about different perspectives. I don't think Mrs. Campbell, my language arts teacher, appreciates my ideas. Actually, I think she's terrified of me. This makes me kind of sad because I don't see myself as a scary guy. I'm swimming a little out of the mainstream, or maybe upstream. Or maybe in a puddle slightly to the left of the stream. But I'm just a little fishy in the great scaly migration we call life, just like everyone else.

Unfortunately, I'm also bored a lot at school because I tend to "get" what the teachers are trying to say before they're finished saying it. So back to how teachers perceive me: They think I'm smart-mouthed and lazy. Hold on folks! There's the other half of the exceptional thing. I have what is formally known as an emotional disability. I tend to react pretty strongly (my teachers would say uncooperatively, rudely, angrily…choose an adverb) when I am frustrated. And I get frustrated a lot because I am bored, or the information in my head is moving too fast, or I can't tie what my brain is saying to what the teacher is saying. As you can imagine, I'm agitated a lot at school, and my teachers generally breathe a sigh of relief when it's time for me to go to the next class.

And I know it. I know people think I'm weird and annoying. For instance, one week I was reading through all of the James Bond books in order. I read pretty fast, as you might have guessed, but when I am into a book I don't like to be distracted. Most kids, when told to put down a book and get to work on their math assignment would comply with only a little grumbling. I sometimes *cannot* do that. It's not that I want to be defiant. Believe it or not, I don't particularly like to draw attention to myself. But when Mr. Tullis asked me to put *Goldfinger* away, my brain said "no." Back to page 287.

A rational person would have said "Shut up brain! I am an upstanding citizen! I am going to listen to the exceptionally smart part of me! Be Gone!" Alas, this was not the case. The full-of-information-eighty-miles-an-hour-can't-stop-can't-refocus-can't-put-the-book-down part of my brain reigned victorious. And that part of my brain came to what seemed a logical conclusion. If I curled up under my desk to read, I wouldn't be bothering Mr. Tullis *or* disrupting the class. So I scrambled not only under the desk, but into the book basket. (I am most comfortable reading in positions that might seem odd to others.) I wedged my head and arms through one side, rested my torso on the algebra textbook, and let my feet stick out the other side. One time, on the Pearl Street Mall, I saw a contortionist yogi-type-guy curl himself into a plastic milk crate. It was impressive. It was cool. It looked painful and exhilarating all at once. I tried to channel that rubber-chicken guy a little bit as I compacted myself beneath my desk. I was very careful not to obstruct the aisle in case of a fire drill, or to subject my neighbors to the aroma of my sweaty feet. I remained quiet throughout this maneuver, and began to read again.

This did not fly with Mr. Tullis. I didn't actually see how he reacted initially as I was engrossed in my book, page 311 to be precise. I did, however, hear him. I was dumped unceremoniously out of my literary reverie by a thundering command of "GET OUT OF MY ROOM YOU DISRESPECTFUL MORON!" It was not uncommon for Mr. Tullis to treat me a bit rudely, but this took the cake. I decided I'd better do what he said. So I started to reverse out of the basket. As luck would have it, the old saying, "You got yourself in, so you can get yourself out" did not hold true here. I could not figure out how to untangle my elbows to escape the dastardly metal cage. The more I twisted the stucker I got, and the more the class giggled. My psychic connection with the contortionist was shattered. This reaction, of course, dramatically increased Mr. Tullis' blood pressure.

Through all of this, I was not trying to be the class clown. I was not trying to get kids to like me. I was definitely not trying to get attention. Everyone in the class was laughing mercilessly at me, and I was really scared. Actually, two people *weren't* laughing. Mr. Tullis was hyperventilating and pounding the red button to call the office like an obsessive-compulsive woodpecker. The other exception, a much more pleasant one, was Lily Tinker.

Lily is a middle school goddess. She is twelve years old, going on thirty. Not that she looks old! Heavens no! She is radiant! She is stunning! She is a paragon of grace and beauty! She is *way* cute. I would say Lily is about five feet tall. She has shoulder-length, wavy strawberry blonde hair that cascades onto her shoulders like spring sunshine. You will have to forgive the cheesy similes here; Lily brings out the romantic poet in me. Her cheeks are a vibrant, rosy pink sprinkled with gingery freckles. And Lily is not a waif. She is not a scrawny little thing like so many of her peers, not trying to emulate some bulimic cover girl. Lily is curvy. She is plump and adorable and divine. Don't stop me now, I'm only just getting started.

Lily is also incredibly intelligent. She always gets 100% on her assignments, and works extremely hard in class. You can tell she always thinks before she speaks because everything that comes out of her mouth is precise and logical. Who cares if her voice sounds a little like a chipmunk? It's what she has to say that matters. And Lily is kind. When someone drops their belongings in the hall, she is the first to scramble to pick them up. If a substitute is struggling to control a class, Lily has been known to actually stand up and tell the kids to knock it off, not because she's a teacher's pet, but because she is a genuinely compassionate human being. I bet she nurses injured squirrels back to health and donates all her free time to working in soup kitchens and stuff like that. That's just the kind of girl Lily is, at least I *think* she is, and I had worshipped her from afar for a really long time. At least two weeks.

And when I got stuck under that desk, Lily did something remarkable. She didn't laugh or point like the other kids. She simply got up out of her desk, marched to the front of the room, grabbed my ankles, and delivered me from my confinement like a stubborn cork from a bottle of bubbly. Well, maybe it wasn't quite that dramatic. But the point is, she saved me from more verbal abuse, from being stuck under that desk forever, and most importantly, from being alone in a moment of crisis.

With a sassy swish of her devastating locks she turned and marched back to her seat, leaving me in a stunned heap of ecstasy on the grimy gray carpet. Mission accomplished. Mr. Tullis and the class were so stunned by her actions that all commotion ceased. I climbed back into my seat, Mr. Tullis inhaled deeply, and class resumed on its intended trajectory.

But how could I concentrate? In that brief, electrifying moment as Lily grasped my bony appendages and liberated me, I had fallen in love. Unfortunately, to Lily I was just an unnatural disaster in need of humanitarian aid. There was no spark for her. But from that moment on, it became my mission, my purpose in life to woo and win Lily Tinker. But how?

For the next few days I worked on my strategy. Should I write her a sonnet? Make her a CD of sappy love songs? Declare my obsession on my web page? Should I send her roses? Offer to carry her books to class? All far too obvious. Lily was much more sophisticated than that. I had to focus. No run-of-the-mill cheesy stunts here. Lily required style.

From my prickly sanctuary, I notice that somewhere in the neighborhood someone is listening to Johnny Cash really loudly. Torture. If I wanted to escape before, it was an imperative now. But wait a second, wasn't Johnny Cash married to someone named Lily? Or maybe I'm thinking of someone else. Maybe that was the name of his horse or his gun or something. FOCUS, BYRON, FOCUS!

So I decided to ask Lily out on a date. Which is what brings me to the present, under this bush, in her front yard, with the dog. What has he been eating? His breath is like decomposing fish guts. But the thing is, I can't stay here forever. I cannot hide from my fate. In order to woo Lily, I must speak to her. With a sigh, I extract the remains of a prehistoric strip of beef jerky and half an Oreo from the pocket of my hoodie. I wave each option in front of him. Not surprisingly, he wags more enthusiastically for the jerky. In one fell swoop I launch the jerky into the grass as far away from the house as possible, and I make a break for it. I reach the front door just as he is realizing that he may well break his canine canines on the "treat" I have produced. No matter. I'm on the front porch. Home free.

A perky wreath of orange and yellow fake flowers surround the hand-painted invitation, "Welcome Friends" on the gleaming white front door. This is encouraging in a Martha-Stewarty sort of way. Deep breath now. Hold it together Byron. (Delve back into history and communicate with your namesake. Be one with the romantic poet.)

I ring the bell.

Lily answers the door. She is wearing pink overalls that stop at her adorable, knobby knees, and a black t-shirt sporting a sequined skull and crossbones. She is barefoot. Her hair is tied back in a casual braid trailing a long hot pink satin ribbon, frayed at the end. There is a smudge of dirt on her right cheek, and a zit emerging on her chin. The morning sun is rising through a window behind her, backlighting her silhouette so it glows like a monster pasted into a bad 1960s horror film. She looks at me and yawns, a gaping, gasping intake of Saturday morning oxygen, closed with the tiniest little hiccupy-burp. Is there anything more beautiful than this girl? Truly?

"Ummm...hi...Byron, right? What are you *doing* here?" Lily is waking up a little now, and she looks puzzled. She's not angry, but she's unsure how to proceed. Me too. Carpe diem, quam minimum credula postero...etcetera.

"Well, Lily...I would like to ask, cordially, reverently, besottedly, if you would accompany me to Scoops for a soda this lovely morning. I believe that you and I have much in common, and I would like to get to know you better." Who is this brazen rascal? Why is he using such ridiculous vocabulary? Does he smell like cat pee and dog drool? Only catastrophe can come of this!

Another yawn. This time she's twirling her braid around her finger and looking vaguely off in the direction of the dog, still masticating the pseudo-meat I'd provided for his culinary pleasure. "Chauncy, get in here!" she commands. The authority in her voice gives me chills. She opens the door to let him in, and turns away from me. I sigh, assuming our brief courtship has come to a premature end. I kick my soggy shoe against the front step to try and release some of the saliva, and turn to go, alternately squishing and scraping down the front walk. As I'm perusing the collection of miniature garden gnomes on either side of the path, the earth stands still for a moment.

"Where are you going? Wait up. I need to grab my flip-flops."

I stagger to a halt, trip on my own foot as I turn around, tumble to the ground, and crush a red-hatted dwarf pushing a wheelbarrow full of plastic daisies. Can I believe my ears?

She's gone, but the door is ajar. In the few seconds it takes me to compose myself, Lily is back. She skips down the steps to meet me, looks quizzically at the gnome carnage at my feet, shrugs, and begins to flip and flop off down the street. Abruptly I realize that I'm expected to go with her. Then my brain kicks in, and I lope along in pursuit of her shadow.

Scoops is only a block and a half away. We don't talk as we walk. Lily looks around, smiling occasionally, soaking up the morning sun. Next door to the shop is the house of one of Asheville's older residents. The breeze this morning is setting the thirty-odd plastic pinwheels in her front yard in motion. They are planted, along with hundreds of plastic daffodils and tulips, in bright green Astroturf. Wind chimes made of silverware, bottle tops, and what appear to be chicken bones perform a cacophonous symphony for our listening pleasure. No HOA here, folks. Did I mention the house is painted lime green? It's like an alternate reality surrounded by a white picket fence so as not to be contaminated by the "real" world.

We enter the store. There are a few kids from A.M.S. already inside. They stop to look and whisper. Lily says hi to them all, oblivious to their curiosity. She orders a lime rickey. Once I manage to close my gaping jaw, I order a cherry Coke. She allows me to pay. Without a word, Lily holds the door for me. She's a modern woman in an age of failed chivalry. We sit at a white metal table in the shade, facing the stunning garden display next door.

Lily takes a long, pensive swig of her beverage then gives a satisfied sigh. It's time to get serious.

"So what's up, Byron? What are we doing here? I mean, this is nice and all. It's a great morning. But...ummmm...I barely even know who you are. Did you want to talk to me about something?"

I can barely breathe. I need a paper bag. I can't remember why

I'm here. Oh yes, undying love! That's it! But I am pretty sure I'm going to pass out. She is talking to me. I focus on a one-legged plastic flamingo staring me down beyond the picket fence, and I speak. To the flamingo, mostly, but I'm aiming in Lily's general direction. The flamingo is much less intimidating.

"Lily, you are a paragon of all that is good and right in this sad and crazy world. You are kind and honest. You are pure and delicate. You are strong and deliberate. You should run for President of these United States. Your voice brings me to my knees in its high-pitched splendor. Your eyes remind me of light captured in the murky creek at twilight. You defend the innocent and the frail. You believe in justice and equality. You are smart, you are witty, and you have *outstanding* iridescent purple toenail polish. (I noticed this on the walk over while focusing on the cracks in the sidewalk.) You have a really interesting dog. And I'm pretty sure you don't hate me. Lily, I have to tell you that I believe I love you, and I will never love another in this way. You are awesome." And all this was said in a single breath. Extremely fast. Lily had her straw in her mouth the whole time, with a gulp of lime rickey held stationary within it for my entire monologue. It wasn't Shakespeare, but it was out. And I could exhale. I waited in terror for Lily's response.

In a fairly disgusting yet impressive display, she released the liquid from the straw back into her glass and began to blow bubbles, all the while looking down at the crusty tabletop. After what seemed like an eternity, she looked up, no flamingo on which to fix her gaze.

"Well, that's really interesting and all, Byron. And it's kind of cool to have a groupie. But...well...I don't love you. In fact, I think you're pretty bizarre. You seem like you're off on your own planet most of the time, you know? All that stuff you just said, that's really nice. I think. It was kind of freaky, too. But the fact is, we are twelve years old. And you are sweet, but maybe you need to join the world that...well...that the rest of us live in?"

"So you're saying this isn't going to work out."

'Um, yeah. Pretty much. But thanks for the soda."

"Is there anything that would change your mind? Anything at all?"

"Well, if you started acting like all the other kids, maybe. But I don't know Byron, it kind of seems to me that you are who you are. We're just not right for each other, you know? When I fall in love, I need to find someone who's a little more...ummm...average."

That's when the ground dropped out from beneath my feet. Someone a little more average. Wow. Lily drained her glass and got up to leave.

'It was ummm...nice hanging out with you this morning, Byron. I'm going to go now. OK?"

"Yeah, sure," I mumbled. "Tell Chauncy I said hi."

Lily bobbed her head slightly and bounced off in the direction of her well-manicured life. And I was alone. Average? What was that supposed to mean? Is that really something to strive for? That was possibly the most devastating adjective I had ever heard. If Lily Tinker was looking for average, our true love was definitely not meant to be. I tried to shake off my disappointment. I left a handful of change on the table as a tip, and I turned to go.

Then something caught my attention, a glimpse of color dropping from the sky out of the corner of my eye. Could it be my mother's life-long dream come to fruition? An alien life form visiting Asheville on a sunny April morning? The movement was occurring in the highly ornamented garden next door, and the object had emerged from the apple tree. The wind chimes had gone crazy with this disturbance, almost deafening in their discord. And the terrestrial being wasn't extra. It was a girl. She was sporting a cape fashioned from a tattered purple beach towel. Her ashy blond hair stood out in curly springs all over her head. She looked to be about my age, and she was not at all perturbed by the fact that I had witnessed her bumbling descent. "What are you looking at?" she demanded in a surprisingly mellifluous voice...warm syrup pouring onto a waffle.

'I was just admiring your entrance," I countered, amazed by my boldness, and by my ability to compose a rational sentence. "It was quite splendid. Do you inhabit that tree often?"

"Only when I'm visiting my Gran. The rest of the time I live with my insane family in Pueblo." Her family was crazy compared to the owner of this house? Curiouser and curiouser. "My name's Elise. Who are you?"

"Byron, Byron Jones," I replied. I leaned over the fence and plucked

13

a tattered fuchsia windmill from the synthetic sod. "May I offer you this token of my esteem, and welcome you to our fine community?"

"Sure. I guess it matches my cape."

"This garden is quite the spectacle," I offered, hoping to keep the conversation going.

"This? Are you kidding? This is nothing. You wouldn't believe the inside of the house. Gran's probably trying to contact Luke Skywalker on my cell right now. You can't pay for that level of entertainment, not even in Vegas." Giggling, she skipped, yes skipped, through the dilapidated storm door and into the shadowy enigma of her home away from home. The moment was lost. I embarked upon my sad and lonely journey home.

About twenty feet down the block it happened. The voices in my head telling me what an idiot I was and how everyone would be laughing at me even more than usual at school on Monday were abruptly drowned out.

"Are you coming or what? She thinks Shakira is Princess Lea. I'm telling you, we could sell tickets."

Parallel universe? Perhaps. But in the end, I guess that's probably right where I belong. Reverse, now, Byron. After all, sometimes the future, paradoxically, lies right behind you.

CROSSING THE DIVIDE

We're in the car and we've just entered the mouth of the Eisenhower Tunnel. My little sister, Maggie, is obsessing over Dora on the TV on the back of my mom's seat. My brother, Alex, slumped over next to her, is drooling, farting, grunting, and snoring pretty much simultaneously, a really attractive combination. My best friend Luke and I are in the back seat, wide awake, and anticipating the freakish phenomenon that we know is about to occur.

If you've never crossed the Continental Divide, it's a truly weird experience. Loveland Pass is fun, but it's even cooler to make the journey through the tunnel. In fact, once when we were halfway through it the lights went out. It was awesome! It was absolutely pitch black, no emergency lights or anything. It only lasted for a couple of seconds, long enough for my sister to scream and my mother to blame the blackout on my dad. (He had nothing to do with it, it was just an automatic response on her part.) It was like knowing for just one moment what it's like to be dead and gone from the world, you know? Crazy stuff.

But the best thing about getting to the other side of the tunnel, other than that whacked out understanding that you're driving under probably thousands of tons of solid mountain with bighorn sheep bouncing around on your head, is the weather when you get out. It doesn't always happen, but it's predictable enough that we hit it at least three or four times a year, regardless of the season. So here's the thing:

15

It could be blazing sun, blue skies, and balmy temperatures on the east side. But about midway into the tunnel the warning signs start flashing, literally: "Slow Down" and "Icy Road Ahead." Unsuspecting tourists seem puzzled by the pulsing, orange digital messages. Ice? Winter? How could that be? Isn't it June? True enough, but the Continental Divide is a crazy place. It's like driving through a portal to another world.

So rented minivans and sporty roadsters slam out the other side at 65 mph and begin to fishtail wildly. Sometimes it's just snizzling out there, a nasty, sloppy mixture of cold rain and wet snow. But other times, you ram straight into a white out, a full on blizzard, even if it was a lovely spring day without a cloud in the sky three miles back. I don't know the scientific explanation for all this, but I do know that it's like the world splits in two.

On the one hand it's kind of funny to watch all the flatland idiots hit their brakes, the worst possible thing you can do on a slick slope. On the other hand, it's kind of scary. You can tell that everyone has moved in a split second from comfort to terror. You can see people tense up in their seats, grab onto the wheel or the door handles, like that's going to avert an accident. And when they hit the brakes, the result is generally to lose control of the car, which can last just a second. Or like the instance we saw last August, your reaction can smash you into the concrete median. Everyone walked away from that one dazed but alive, but I bet that's not always the case.

Luke and I are always ready for a show when we get to the other side, never sure what might happen. It's kind of funny, because he's my best friend. He has been since we were three. But right now I'm feeling like I've been on the uphill approach to the tunnel for ten years and just came out into a storm on the other side that I didn't know was there. I had no clue. Because after practically being brother and sister through all of elementary school and into middle, I've suddenly learned something about Luke. Something that maybe everyone else has known for a while. Apparently, Luke is possibly, maybe, probably gay.

So we're sitting here, not talking, which isn't all *that* unusual. We take this trip to my parents' condo in Silverthorne once every couple of months, and it gets boring chatting the whole way. But this time is different. It's like an invisible wall has come up between us. I don't know what to say or how to act, and I really don't know what to do next.

He wrote me a letter, not an email, last week. He was afraid that someone would get a hold of it electronically and then everyone would know. But he was also afraid to talk to me in person about it. And I haven't responded at all. Great friend, huh? This trip has been planned for a while, and we're just going along, acting like nothing has happened between us. But it seems like somehow everything has to change now. Doesn't it?

What he wrote is that he's suspected something was different for him for a long time. Sure, Luke has always hung out with girls more than guys, but so what? He's sweet. Is that a crime? We love him because he listens to us. He helps us with our hair and our makeup. He gossips with us about the guys we like. None of this ever occurred to me as out of the ordinary until he pointed it out. I guess we've been this way, this close, for so long that I'm kind of oblivious to anything outside of the little bubble that is my life. In elementary sometimes boys would make fun of Luke for hanging out with us, but they would make fun of *us* too for hanging out with him, so who knew?

And in middle school, where everything gets scarier and harder for everyone, where no one knows who they can trust for at least that first year, all I knew was that I still had Luke, and he was my best friend, and he would always be there. I did my share of crying in 6th and 7th grade. I got bullied some for looking tomboy-ish, for being quiet, those sorts of things. Luke was always the one I ran to, to cry on his shoulder. He always listened and hugged and made me feel better. It never occurred to me that he might need me for the same reason. Luke is always, even now, giggly and happy and fun. He can make the worst situation seem like no big deal. I've always taken for granted that he will take care of *me*, not the reverse.

To give you a taste of the goofiness of Luke's personality, take the duck incident. We were spending the day at the zoo with my family a few weeks ago. A small group of onlookers had gathered to watch a massive polar bear lumbering around in its scummy pond when a particularly clueless duck flapped down into the enclosure. What happened next was like a scene from Animal Planet. The polar bear suddenly perked up and bolted across the rocks faster than any of us

17

knew such a critter could travel. Its target: The unsuspecting duck. Just inches before the bear's gaping jaws snapped up a feathery snack, the duck came to its senses and made an impressive vertical lift-off away from impending doom. All this time, Luke had been in near hysterics about saving the duck. Couldn't anyone do something? Where was the zoo keeper? This was so not ok! Things along that line. Luke is nothing if not an outstanding drama queen.

In his frenzy to save the duck, Luke apparently tuned out all other auditory and visual information. Once the duck gained altitude, it made an abrupt 90 degree turn and beelined towards us quacking wildly. The spectators all began to scream "Duck!" as the bird flew straight at our heads, and most of us, logically, dropped to the ground. Luke, still obsessing over the welfare of his feathered friend, started screaming "Yes, it's a duck! Fly away little duck! Be free! Go, go go!" completely missing the point that the screams from the peanut gallery were a command *to duck* not to *cheer on the duck*. The result? Luke ended up with the duck's feet hopelessly tangled in his hair, screaming like…well…a girl, and flailing his arms around like a demented windmill. When we all got back on our feet and dislodged the bird, Luke's reaction was, "Is it hurt? Is the duck ok? Do we need to take it to a vet?" That's Luke for you. He is sensitive to the end, and doesn't think twice about what people think when he reacts the way it's natural for him to react. He is kind and caring and so, so easily hurt.

And now here we are. I have his letter folded up in about a hundred neat creases in the pocket of my jeans. I've read it about that many times, too. But I haven't said a word. And I've got to do something soon, because Luke is the most amazing person in the world, and if I don't respond, I am the worst person ever. But I just don't know what to say.

Luke said in the letter that the thing that made him "see the light," of all things, was American Superstar. Get the laughter out of your system, I'm being serious. He and I have watched intently since 4th grade. We are vicious critics, usually agreeing with everything the crabbiest judge has to say. But that is our private time. We plop down in my basement religiously from January to May with a bag of popcorn and just veg out. It's just the way it is. I'm not claiming it's quality programming, but it's what we do. It's our chance to judge rather than be judged, but without hurting anyone's feelings. A win-win situation.

So Luke introduced his situation to me by saying that it has occurred to him this season that the only contestants he finds cute at all are the boys. In particular, he admits, Corey Lopez gives him goose bumps. When that skinny, strawberry-blonde, shrieky sensation hits the stage, Luke apparently gets weak at the knees. And when he started thinking about it more carefully, he realized that none of the female contestants were catching his eye. So he started to think outside the world of reality programming and realized that this was not a case of being star-struck. When he notices people's appearances at school, apparently it's always boys, unless it's to compliment a girl on her outfit or her new shadow color, that sort of thing. Then he started digging even deeper, and came to notice that at night, when he's having those private little thoughts, those crazy scenarios about people you'd like to graze hands with, to make eye contact with, or dare we say, *kiss*, they were all the same gender as Luke. So the final test, he said in the letter, was me. I'm not really sure how to feel about this, and it's making me pretty uncomfortable I have to admit, but here it is.

Luke admitted that when he stops to think about me, his soul mate, his partner in crime, his psychic twin for eight years, if he's being honest, I do not make his heart flutter even a little bit. Now this is something that I guess had never really occurred to me, a romantic connection with Luke. Sure, I've had crushes before. I have gone to a couple of school dances with a couple of different guys, usually theater nerds like me, and had a few fairly inappropriate text conversations.

But Luke? Yes, he's my perfect match in pretty much every way, but I'd never considered anything beyond friendship until he brought it up. So the point is this: When forced to do so, when Luke brought up the topic, I realized that yes, if the situation arose I would date him. But the situation hasn't arisen, and it looks like it won't. And that's ok with me, and it's also not the point. The point is that when Luke asked himself the same question, his answer was no. There is no possibility of a spark, not even a glimmer of hope for us to hook up. And that *freaked him out* because we love each other, we really do. It's an absolute, undying commitment, just not of the Romeo and Juliet variety. It's more like, well, Harry and Hermione. You get the idea.

So when Luke forced himself to admit that that type of relationship would not work for him, he knew there was a problem. At least he's referring to it as a problem, his word choice, not mine. If he couldn't imagine hooking up with me, the person he is closest to in the world, then something was definitely up. So he drops this bomb on me. He likes boys. And he's *really, really* scared.

Let me give you a little more context here, because Luke doesn't necessarily fit the immediate stereotypes you might have for a gay teenager. He's actually a math and science geek. He dresses the part, looks the part. Button down shirts and jeans, wire-framed glasses slipping down the nose, messy hair. He's not a "pretty boy" by any means, not particularly girly. Granted, he's a bit of a fashion snob when it comes to his girl friends, but he pays absolutely no attention to his own clothes. His shirt is almost always hanging half out of his pants. His shoes are often untied. And he generally clashes pretty horrifically. Luke's not a boy who you would look at and automatically assume he was batting for the other team.

He is, however, pretty outgoing, and popular, too. He has always been kind of a class clown, but not the kind that drives the teacher crazy. The teachers generally *love* Luke. He can completely destroy a class, quoting from Monty Python in character, for example, reducing everyone to hysterics, and the teachers laugh right along side. He's just got that kind of personality that draws people to him. He's a little flamboyant, lots of hand gestures and dramatic voices, but I always assumed that was just his unique style. Fortunately for him, his friendliness has won over pretty much everyone in the school. Maybe this will help in the next few years.

Luke's family is really cool, and very open. They talk about all sorts of stuff at the dining room table, and contrary to my family, they actually all sit down and have dinner together *every* night. It's really fun. They talk about religion, politics, the state of the world, the Simpsons, you name it. I've always loved going over there to eat. It's like no topic is off limits. You can bring up absolutely anything and not be cut down for it. Luke's parents are totally divided, for example, on global warming, and the debates are amazing! One night his mom actually threw a roll at his dad for calling Al Gore a middle-aged pseudo-academic couch potato. You have to love it.

But in the letter, Luke told me that I wasn't the first person he'd told the big secret. After a round of post-inaugural Hillary versus Barack banter last week, between the Caesar salad and the free-range grilled chicken, Luke dropped the bomb. He honestly didn't think his parents would react too strongly, and at first they didn't. He says it got *really* quiet for a minute, then his younger brother, Casey, said, "So what? What are you so happy about?" At that point Luke says there was a general sigh of relief and the matter was dropped. Just like that.

But he was actually kind of crushed. He was hoping his parents would jump up and congratulate him and hug him or something. They're pretty liberal about most things, so he was assuming that this would really be no different. He wasn't counting on silence.

A couple of days passed before the list appeared. Again at dinner, with Casey off at a friend's house, the topic came up. Luke was kind of blindsided when his parents presented a bullet-pointed list of the top ten reasons Luke wasn't gay. Seriously, he didn't copy the whole list for me, but they were trying to turn it into a joke, like a segment from a late show. It included things like "#7: Because you dress like the PC guy on the Mac commercials" and ironically "#1: Because Annie (that's me, by the way) will never marry you." I guess they were sort of nervously giggling the whole time his dad read him the list, trying to be all casual and silly. His mom closed the conversation by assuring Luke he was just going through a phase and that he should just keep his thoughts to himself until they passed. They said it would be easiest and safest for Luke that way.

They offered to get Luke some counseling if he wanted it, to help him "get back on track." You have to understand that this is coming from two parents who go and see *Rent* every time it comes to town, who whooped and hollered when Ellen came out of the closet. You get the picture. They're all about people's right to live their lives, just not Luke. Don't get me wrong, I think they're really good, kind people at heart, not raging hypocrites. I can only imagine what they were thinking when Luke broke the news.

Flashback to when Luke and I were about 4 years old, screaming into the house from an excellent snowball fight, only to come to a dead standstill when we found his mom leaning on the kitchen counter, sobbing quietly, listening to some random guy talking on the radio. We

21

didn't understand at the time why Luke's mom was so upset. When he asked her about it years later, it turns out that there was a breaking story about Matthew Shepherd being murdered. She just couldn't believe, she told Luke, how cruel people could be for no good reason. Luke asked her about this earlier this year, when we were running inside, *again* from a different snowball fight and he happened to recall that day. I bet Luke's parents got a pretty vivid reality check when he broke the news.

After the list, it was Luke's turn to get really quiet. He asked to be excused, went to his room, and started writing to me. Which brings us to this point. I just found out that my best friend is gay, his parents want to "fix" him, and he's ready to crawl right back into the closet. I want to be able to help him somehow, to support him, to make him understand that I don't care whether he likes boys or girls as long as he still likes me. How do I say all that to him without making him feel weird? Right now, I guess I just don't, because we've been in this car for an hour and haven't said anything but "hi."

There are a lot of things I'm wondering, things I would like to ask him. Does being gay mean he's going to start dressing differently? Will he start hanging out with new people at school? And the question I'm the most worried about in the end is, will he still hang out with me? Will Luke still be my best friend even though his world has turned upside down? I guess that more than anything I'm afraid I might lose him.

But at the same time, I'm kind of afraid to be seen with him. Does that make me a bad person? It's not like I'm this insanely popular kid. I have a few friends, and I mostly try to exist underneath everyone's radar, to not get noticed a whole lot. If Luke decides to announce to the world that he likes boys, what will people think of me? Will they assume that I'm gay too? I love Luke to death. I really do. I would throw myself in front of a train for him. But would I throw myself to the mercy of a pack of rabid thirteen years olds? I don't know. I just don't know if I'm strong enough for that. I'm being honest, and it makes me feel so ashamed.

And what if Luke's parents are right? What if people *do* want to hurt him? I looked up Matthew Shepherd on Wiki after Luke got the story from his mom. I saw those pictures of that baby-faced guy and that fence post, and I read the story over and over again from a Laramie newspaper archive. It's not right to treat an animal that way, let alone a human being. What I learned made me sick to my stomach. If there are people out there who hate you like that, way down in their guts, just for being who you are, what chance does Luke have? He is this amazing, compassionate, funny, beautiful person, and people have a right to despise him even if they've never met him? It makes my brain hurt even thinking about that.

Now we're coming to the end of the tunnel. That kind of fizzy orange glow is fading into natural light. I'm running out of time to hide. We're almost to the condo. As we emerge from the shadows, Luke looks over at me and cracks a smile for the first time all day. No snow today, no sleet. Rain is coming down in torrents, like someone is literally sitting up there on the side of the mountain dumping buckets out. But we have to have a *little* meteorological fun, right? So here it is. My dad can barely see through the windshield because of the volume of water. The wipers can't even keep up. *But the sun is out.* It is illuminating the road like a spotlight, somehow, and at the same time we're getting the car washed for the first time in several months. This is new and different. This is interesting. This is kind of entertaining, at least from the passenger's point of view.

The windows are fogging up now. Luke reaches over me and starts to scribble, like a condensation Etch-a-Sketch artist. It's dripping as he writes, dissolving almost as fast as the image takes shape. But I can tell that he's drawn a heart, and in the middle is just one word: Annie.

So what else can I do? I have no choice. I punch him in the arm, hard. Then I lean my head on his shoulder and whisper, "Me too. Yeah. Me too."

Room 100

Let's be real. There ain't nothing cool about playing a trombone. Nothing at all. It was like kissing a buzzing bee made of tinfoil, and no matter how I tried, I could not get the right notes to come out. I would slide that thing back and forth, back and forth, and still it sounded like I was pulling on an elephant's tail, not making any kind of music. And that's embarrassing. Every time any kind of a noise came out of it everybody in that band room turned to stare at me. They rolled their eyes, some of them laughed, and they all looked around at each other like I was a joke. And I guess they were probably right. I had no business being in that room, not even for a second.

Mr. Jones agreed. He kept me after class a few times to try and help me learn, and he was pretty nice and all, but he didn't get it. I didn't want to learn the stupid trombone. I wanted to be out of that spotlight, and fast. So I gave him some lip, talked back when he tried to show me how to play. That's how I operated when I wanted to escape, and most of the time, it worked just great. So what happened next? Mrs. Sobol, the counselor lady, she told me that I was getting a new elective instead of band. And that's exactly what I wanted. Until she told me what I was taking instead. It went down like this.

"We have no electives with room for you at the moment, Alex. But since you have *chosen* not to succeed in band, we need to find you a home for the rest of the year. So you're going to be a teacher's aide in room 100," she said with a lot of sighing and flipping of her bleached-out hair.

"Room 100? What's that? What do I got to do?" I asked. The way she said it made it sound like the hotel room you do not want to go into in the bad horror movie. I was pretty sure this was not going to be fun. If it was art or computer tech she would have just handed me a schedule, right?

"Room 100 is where the children with special needs take most of their classes. They need some students their own age to help them with classroom activities and to play with them at recess. This is what you will be doing for the remainder of the year during period 7. Starting tomorrow."

I started to complain, but then I caught myself. There was that stupid trombone, or there was a room full of the kids who are hidden away from the rest of the school. Some of them yelled and screamed in the hallways and hit out at their teachers. Some of them had special food. Some of them needed help in the bathroom. None of these things sounded too great to me. But, some of them got to ride the elevator, and *that* was cool. So there it was. A choice between band and helping in the "special" class. That was a no brainer.

So I started going to room 100 every day. At first, I did *not* like it. I didn't know what to do. Some of the kids would come up to me and try and touch me, or talk to me, but I couldn't understand what they were trying to say. It freaked me out, those kids trying to grab on to me. I didn't know then that there was nothing to be afraid of, but I was going to learn. Henry and Mrs. Cash helped me figure that one out.

Henry was the first kid I met in room 100. He used words I could understand most of the time, and he asked *a lot* of questions. That's more than I could say for a lot of the kids. But I guess they probably thought *I* was pretty weird because I didn't want to talk all the time. I'm a pretty quiet guy, you know.

"What your name?"

"Alex."

"What your name?"

"I said Alex, man."

"*What your name?*"

"Leave me alone, dude!" Henry was grabbing at my arm and

shaking it and I was backing into the corner. He had some drool dripping down his face from the corner of his mouth, and was getting real bothered about something. I figured I could sneak out and hide in the bathroom for the period, but before I could make a break for it, Mrs. Cash stopped me.

"He wants to know your *whole* name," she told me. Turned out Mrs. Cash was one of the grown up teacher-helpers in the room who helped kids in the bathroom and cleaned them up after lunch, that kind of thing. But right then, I didn't know her, so I didn't say a word, just looked on down at my shoes.

So she kept right on talking.

"Henry is super-friendly. He likes to know as much as he can about who he's talking to. He's not a shy boy," she explained.

"Ummm...ok. I'm Alex. Alex Christopher Payne," I whispered.

"Nice to meet you, Alex. Henry, this is Alex Christopher Payne. He's a 6th grader, just like you."

Henry wiped his hand on his jeans and held it out to me. Great.

"I am Henry David Rieder. I live at 20084 West 40th Street. My favorite color is green. I like to eat pizza and play video games. Are you my best friend now?"

I could figure out all of his words, but he talked kind of funny, like he had a whole bunch of food stuck in his mouth. What was I supposed to say? I was going to be in here for 45 minutes, and that was it. And he just wiped drool on his pants so he wouldn't get it on my hand.

But then I thought about band again, and I gave up. Mrs. Cash was kind of giggling this whole time, like there was some real funny joke going on that I didn't understand. I held out my hand to Henry. He grabbed it and shook it so hard that I swear I heard a couple of bones break.

"Hey, man, let go already!" I yelled. Henry smiled at me with this huge mouthful of teeth that filled up just about his whole head.

"Sorry, sorry, Alex," he said. Then he started to jump up and down hollering, "This is my best friend, Alex! This is my best friend, Alex, everyone! Right here! Look! My best friend!"

Now I was turning tomato red and all I wanted to do was hide under a table.

'It's all right, Alex. This is a big compliment. Henry hasn't picked a new best friend in at least two days," Mrs. Cash grinned.

"What's his problem, ma'am?" I asked.

"No problem, but he does have Downs Syndrome if that's what you're asking."

"What's that about?"

"Well, it means a lot of different issues for a lot of different people, but for Henry it means that he's learning just about like a third grader, and he isn't going to grow much bigger than he is right now, among other things." I didn't ask what those other things were. I was pretty sure I didn't want to know.

"Alex, will you come over to my house to play?" Henry said.

No way was I going to be seen with this kid in public. *No way.* Hanging out in here was one thing, but outside? Uh-uh.

"Relax, Henry. You have to give people a chance to get to know you. Why don't you show Alex what you've been working on this week?"

"Ok, ok," he said. He grabbed my hand (again) and dragged me over to this table covered in pictures. Some were big old glittery messes, some looked like fingerpaints. But Henry pointed to one that I could actually figure out. It was a picture of a lady and a man pushing a little baby in a stroller. It was a colored pencil drawing, and it was good, *really* good. There were trees that looked like trees and the people actually looked like people. There was a house in the background that was better than anything I could draw.

"You did this?" I asked him.

"Yeah. Henry draws this. Henry wants to get married when he grows up and have a beautiful baby boy. That's what Henry wants," he answered.

I looked over at Mrs. Cash. She shrugged and said, "Henry knows what he wants. That's more than most people can say."

I guess that was true. I sure didn't know what I wanted for dinner that night, let alone for the rest of my life. This little Henry dude was kind of growing on me. Maybe hiding in the bathroom wasn't such a hot idea. I sat at the art table with Henry for the rest of the period while he drew another picture, this time of his trip to the zoo the last weekend. It was pretty decent, too. I could actually tell what was a zebra and what was a lion. When I drew animals they all looked like

27

deformed dogs. All's I could draw good was cars. But Henry? Looked like he could draw just about anything. I was pretty impressed about that. In fact, the bell rang for 8th period before I even knew it was time to go. Room 100 wasn't so bad after all.

After school I was messing around with my cousin Freddy in the parking lot. I smacked him in the back of the head with my math binder, so he kicked me in the privates. I was busy curling up in a ball on the ground when Dean Barron kicked us off school property.

"You want to impede your future as a parent, do it at your apartment, not here!" she screamed. I didn't know exactly what she meant, but I had a pretty good guess. Freddy pulled me up, and we ran for the bus. But as usual, it was pulling away when we got there. Freddy ran up and pounded on the door, but the driver sped up. He didn't like us too well. So we started walking. Lucky for us, it was a nice day. The sun was out, and it wasn't too cold. Still not as warm as Texas, but not too bad. We made it home in a half hour. My mom yelled at us for being late while she ran around trying to get dressed for her class that night. She was in school to be a helper in a hospital, so she stayed with my little brother and sister during the day, and then took off as soon as I got home with Freddy.

After she left, I turned on some cartoon for Larissa and Michael. I crashed on the couch while Freddy talked to his girl on his phone. Then I got the kids some cereal and juice for dinner. I made them pee and brush their teeth, then I put them to bed. As long as we were staying with my Aunt Stephanie, there wasn't a whole lot of extra room. I slept on the couch, and Freddy slept in his bed in the room with the little guys. Right after I turned out the light, Stephanie got home. She fixed a frozen pizza for me and Freddy, but she said she wasn't hungry. She worked late most nights as a teller at a bank, and she found out last week she was going to have a baby. Her feet and her back hurt all the time, and she talked a lot about where were we going to put another kid in this dump. The apartment was busting already with beds and clothes and toys. I guess that was why they were talking about leaving.

I heard my mom one night talking about going back to Houston. She said she could make some good money out there, and Grandma and Granpop could take care of the kids. I have to say, getting to eat

Grandma's menudo whenever I wanted would be ok by me. But we moved to Denver in October. Now it was February. This was the longest I'd ever stayed in a school. My mom was real young, only a couple years older than me, when she had me. She'd been "Looking for Mr. Right," so she said, for all these years, someone to take care of us. Along the way, Mr. Wrong gave her Larissa and Michael, a busted jaw, a couple of maxed out credit cards, and some nights in jail. So now she was talking about going back to her mom and dad and getting a fresh start. If you asked me, I'd say she was lucky Grandma and Granpop would take us back at all. But whatever. I was used to not going to school, or not going for long. Every time we showed up somewhere new I was further and further behind all the other kids, so I mostly just didn't bother to try. What was the point?

Stephanie went to bed right after we ate. Freddy stayed up watching TV with me until around midnight, then I curled up under that ratty old Spongebob blanket on the couch. I heard my mom come in a while later, but I pretended to be asleep. Most nights I didn't want to know what she did after class anyways.

The next day, the kids from room 100 went outside to play kickball. There was a lot of screaming. Kids were tripping over their own feet. Some were crying because they didn't want to play, or they didn't want to lose, or they wanted to go have a snack. It was kind of like being with my kid brother and sister. I don't usually do sports, but Henry really wanted me to play. So when he kicked the ball, I ran alongside him. I kept tripping on my pants, and I had to hold them up with one hand.

"Where do you *get* pants that big, Alex?" yelled Mrs. Cash. I didn't answer her. I wore what I wanted, and this looked cool. She just didn't know style, that's all.

But it did make it hard to run. I was way slower than Henry, so he stopped every couple feet to yell, "This is my best friend! My best friend Alex Christopher Payne! He likes menudo and rap music! His pants are falling off his butt! He's my best friend!" It was pretty embarrassing, but we finally arrived at first base. I decided that the next day I would put on a belt and maybe some rubber bands around my ankles to hold my pants up so I could run a little better.

Then Mrs. Cash was up to kick. A kid named Gracie sent her the ball, and it actually was rolling pretty fast. Mrs. Cash swung back her leg and nailed that ball. It flew high above the football field towards the gym. But it wasn't the only thing in the air. When Mrs. Cash's leg kicked up, it flew off. No joke. The whole bottom half of her leg shot out of her jeans and went spinning through the air at top speed, then crashed down about two feet away from Marty Peel. Marty took one look at the leg and started to bawl. I let out a string of cuss words before I could even think, and Henry copied every one at the top of his lungs. Everyone just stood there for a second, then one of the teachers, Mr. Watson, bolted over to Mrs. Cash. I expected her to be screaming and crying and gushing blood, but when I got up the nerve to look over there, that woman was *laughing. What?*

Mr. Watson had his arm around her waist and was helping her sit down on the ground. I finally got some guts and ran over there as fast as I could with my pants dangling like they always did. I pulled out my phone. "Mrs. Cash, I'm calling 911. Don't worry. The ambulance is coming!" I screamed. I was freaking out, and Henry was jumping up and down beside me like a kangaroo.

I figured she must have been in shock. She was laughing so hard there were tears running down her cheeks. But when I looked over at Mr. Watson, he was standing there holding his belly, and he was laughing too. "What is the problem with you people?" I yelled. "Mrs. Cash needs a doctor. And someone needs to go get that leg. If we save it, they can sew it back on at the hospital. I saw that on TV. Henry! Go get Mrs. Cash's leg from center field, RIGHT NOW!"

Henry looked at me with this pout like I'd asked him to clean his room for the 100th time. "But Alex, I had to go get the leg *last* time. Today it's Gracie's turn," he argued.

"And Alex, we don't need a doctor to put it back on," Mrs. Cash snorted. "I can do it myself!"

"Are you people *crazy?* This is an emergency right here! You're all acting like someone lost a tooth or something! Mrs. Cash, *you are missing a leg!*" I was in a big panic now. Was I dreaming all this? Then Gracie wandered over, and she was carrying…well…the leg. But there was no blood dripping from it, no bones or guts sticking out. She handed the leg over to Mrs. Cash. She hiked up her jeans to her knee, and I saw that her real leg ended right there in a shiny stump. In the space where her calf and her foot should have been, there was only air. Without a word, Mrs. Cash pulled the flying leg up against her knee, hard. There was a "pop" like the sound of pulling a plunger out of a nasty toilet, and the leg stuck to her knee, just like that.

"Sometimes when I get a little too energetic I snap the suction on it, Alex. It's no big deal. It doesn't hurt, I promise." Mrs. Cash put her hands on the grass and pushed herself up to her feet. She stretched her leg a little, bent it a few times, then walked in a couple of small circles. "That's better. It's in exactly the right position now," she sighed.

I was so mad. I looked at Mrs. Cash, then Mr. Watson, then Henry, and then I turned around and spat on the ground. "Why didn't anybody tell me you had fake parts that could come undone if you looked at them funny? Huh? Why not? You people are going to hide something like that? Joke about it? What else do I need to know about this freak show?" I demanded. Nobody answered me. "I'm out of here," I said. "Who knows what could happen. Next you'll be telling me that Henry is a space alien or something. This is like the circus, man."

I marched off towards the cafeteria door, not looking back. But Henry caught me. He stood right in front of me with both his pant legs hitched up to his thighs. "What are you doing little man? Get out of my way, now. I'm done with this place."

"But Alex Christopher Payne, look! Henry's not hiding secrets! These are my very own legs! Right here! I wish I had a flying leg like Mrs. Cash, but I don't She was in a car accident. Not me. I have two legs here. Right here. No secret legs. Please come back and play, Alex. Please?" He was crying now. When I kept walking, he dropped down on his knees, and then curled up into a little ball right there on the grass. Whatever. These people were laughing at me, and no way I could trust them. Time to go.

That afternoon when I got home I set the kids up with Sesame Street then I went outside to get some air. I was sitting at the top of the stairs with my legs dangling over the edge when Mrs. Cash showed up. She was driving a lime green VW bug, the old-fashioned kind, but all fancy like she took real good care of it. I didn't know what to do. Teachers weren't supposed to come to your house, right? I thought

31

about taking off, but the kids were inside by themselves. And where would I go?

"Hey, Alex," she called up at me. She had a white paper bag in her hand. "Can I come up? I promise I won't lose any limbs this time."

I shrugged my shoulders and turned my back to her. I heard her coming up the stairs, no different than the sound of two regular legs, just one after the other, one after the other. Then she was standing next to me. She put the bag down by the apartment door.

"I brought you some menudo. I'm sure it's not as good as your grandma's, but the guy who owns the restaurant seems to know his stuff. There are some tacos in there for your brother and sister, too."

"How did you know about Larissa and Michael?" I said, not looking up at her.

"Henry told me. Sounds like you two have had some pretty good talks this past week. He really looks up to you, you know. He tells me you're going to be a mechanic when you get out of school. He wants to come and work for you when you own your own garage some day."

"He could come work for me," I said under my breath. "I trust Henry. He's not like most of the grown-ups I know. He's a good kid."

"Can I tell you something Alex?" She waited. "Well, I'm going to tell you whether you want to hear or not. You're a lucky kid."

"What are you talking about? We live in this dump, my mom's never home, we got nothing to do, and we're moving again. What's lucky about that? You don't know nothing, Mrs. Cash."

She was real quiet for what seemed like a long minute, then she let out this big old sigh. "Alex, when I was thirteen, I was riding shotgun in my dad's jeep. He was driving through a green light, not speeding, at 3:30 in the afternoon. He had the day off work and had picked me up from school. We were going to get ice cream. I hardly ever got to spend any time with him. He was a construction worker, and it seemed like he was on site 24-7. I was so excited that day. It was just the two of us.

"As we were passing through that intersection, a red pick-up truck screamed around the corner a block down to our right and ran the light. It plowed into the side of the jeep. If I hadn't been wearing my seatbelt, I would probably be dead right now. The jeep flipped over three times. My leg was crushed, and the windshield was smashed into my dad's head. He died before the ambulance arrived. I was conscious in that jeep as he bled to death, Alex, but there was not a thing I could do. I think about him every single day, and it happened more than twenty years ago.

"For a lot of years I thought I would rather be dead than be without my dad. The guy who hit us walked away from that wreck with a few cuts and bruises. All I could think about was how unlucky I was and how terrible my life was. It took me a long time to get over the feeling that life couldn't possibly get any worse.

"But about ten years ago I started working in room 100. After a while of working with kids like Henry, I started to notice something. Some of those kids won't live past their teens, Alex, did you know that?"

I shrugged my shoulders again, but the truth was, I didn't know that. "Henry?" I asked. I was listening for real now.

"No, Henry will live to be an adult, but he'll probably end up in a group home if he's lucky. His parents are older, and they're not going to be around forever. Henry can talk a good game, but he'd have a hard time living by himself. Then there's Gracie, who is pretty much always in pain, and Devin who can understand every word we say but can't speak. And Seth who will always have to get his meals through a tube, and Cat who is slowly going blind. Working with these kids kind of changed my perspective, you know? I started to realize that I was lucky to be alive, to have my mom, and to have one good leg. I was lucky to have a future that didn't involve too much suffering and uncertainty. The past's over. Room 100 taught me how important it is to live for today. Does that make sense?"

I didn't answer, but I was pretty busy thinking over what she had said.

"Well, I'd better leave you to your dinner," she said. "I imagine cold menudo is *not* a good thing. Oh, but Alex?"

"What?" I grumbled.

"Henry misses you like you would not believe. I sure wish you'd reconsider. No one was making fun of you, Alex. You get to laugh with us because you're a part of our family now. That's all." She reached down and mussed my hair, then jogged off down the stairs. Well, she kind of hobble-jogged, but that missing leg just didn't really slow her down.

Later, after I fed the kids and got them to bed, I sat down on the couch and got to some thinking. Maybe I should give room 100 a second chance. It was kind of hard for me to believe that they really wanted me there, and that they weren't just messing with me. Most of my days in school it seemed like people were pointing at me because they were thinking I was dumb, or illegal, or whatever. No one laughed at me down there, and that was all right.

I crashed out and dreamed about all of us in room 100 pulling off our legs and having a contest to see how far we could throw them. I won in that dream, but Henry was a close second. Crazy stuff. At the end of the contest we all hopped around hugging each other then sat down and ate menudo. But then the sound of my mom coming in the door woke me up. I sat up fast and tried to adjust my eyes to the light she'd turned on.

"Good news tonight, mijo, good news!" she whispered at me, but I could tell she was all excited.

"What, Ma?" I mumbled. "I want to sleep."

"Sure, sure, but first let me tell you the plan!"

Plan? What plan? What was she talking about? I was still halfway in my dream and it was real hard to focus my brain on her words.

"We're leaving, Alex, and we're going to be rich! I've figured out a way to make lots of money from these nursing classes. Forget Texas, now. We're all moving to Vegas next week. Apartments are cheap, and your auntie and I will have work right away. How does that sound? Las Vegas, baby!"

Sometimes my mom sounds more like my big sister than a grown up. She doesn't make a bit of sense, and she changes her mind about every ten minutes without thinking things through. Things were going ok here. The apartment was small, but we were all right. There was some food on the table every night. And school? Well, school wasn't so bad some days. I actually had a couple of C's instead of my usual F's. Vegas? For real?

"Why, Ma? That's the dumbest thing I ever heard!" I was awake now, and I was mad. Who was this little girl, this not-even-thirty-year-old trying to pretend to care about us kids? Moving to some strange place with no friends sounded like no plan at all to me. "Forget you. I'm staying here. I'll go live with Fernando or Marcus. No way am I going. Nuh-uh," I screamed.

Now the kids were crying and all the lights were on. People were yelling in the apartment next door for us to shut up. Seemed like wherever we went we were disturbing somebody, and I was *sick* of it. I wanted to fit in for once, be part of the crowd instead of the one getting kicked to the curb.

"You got no choice, mijo. We're leaving next week. I need you to take care of the kids after school when I'm working. You understand? You want them to be by themselves all night?"

Larissa and Michael were standing in the door to their room rubbing their eyes, and they heard that loud and clear. Larissa started sobbing and Michael ran up and attached himself to my leg like gum to a shoe. "No Alex, don't leave us! No! No! No!" he cried. So how was I supposed to handle that? Of course I couldn't leave them, not with my mom in charge. Who knew what would happen.

I gave him a little smack on the head, not a mean one, then I hugged him close. I pulled Larissa over and yanked her up on my lap. I'm not real good at taking care of them, but I guess it's better than nothing. The three of us curled up on the couch together while my mom hit the shower so she could go out to the bar for a while. Larissa and Michael fell asleep on me like a couple of little puppies. I got to admit, it was warm and safe right there. I would do my best with them, even in Las Vegas. But I couldn't help wondering as I tried to get back to that flying-leg dream. Who would take care of Henry? And as I drifted off into a fog of my mom's cigarette smoke and hairspray fumes, I couldn't help wondering if anyone would ever think about taking care of me.

Next day I was back to my routine in room 100. Funny thing was, that place was starting to feel more like home than the apartment. There were always people to talk to, food to eat, and it was pretty much always *loud*. I never liked it when a situation was dead quiet. That always made me feel sure a storm was coming, like that one second where all the birds stop singing before thunder and lightning break loose. No noise meant trouble down the road, no doubt.

So when I opened the front door that afternoon, I knew right away there was a problem. The TV and the lights were off. The kids weren't running around hollering at each other and throwing junk. There was just empty silence like I was the only person left in the world.

And as it turned out, that was kind of true. I thought maybe they'd all gone out somewhere, but my mom never took the kids anywhere. They were always just planted in front of some show or other. I looked in the bedrooms, but no one was there. And there was something else weird. The closets were open, and there were piles of clothes lying around all over the floor, more like a bomb had gone off than usual. By then I was freaking out a little. Maybe somebody had robbed the place and kidnapped everyone. But what kind of a fool would rip junk off from a dump like this? I ran into the kitchen to grab the phone. That's when I saw the note.

My mom's handwriting looks like most of the girls' in my classes, all round and bubbly with big old circles on top of the letter "i" and all that. Her note was just one long line with no capital letters or periods or nothing:

alex we went to texas to borrow some money from grandma we'll be back in a few days there's some frozen dinners in the freezer don't worry about us mom

That was the lightning strike right there. They'd all just gone and left me behind. I didn't care if it was only for a day or two. What kind of mom does that kind of crap? And what happened to Vegas? I scrunched the note up and threw it across the room. Then I turned and smashed my fist so hard into the kitchen wall that the plaster cracked. When I pulled my hand away there was blood coming out of a nasty cut on my knuckles. I stormed out the front door, slamming it behind me so it shook. If they could just up and leave, well so could I.

I ran hard for a while until I got a serious pain in my side. It was starting to get dark, and a little snow was coming down and sticking to my hoodie. I left so fast that I didn't think to grab my jacket. Once I slowed down a little, I started to come to my senses. What was I supposed to do now? Somehow, my brain flipped onto autopilot, and my feet followed. I passed 38th, then 39th, turned right on 40th. After a few more blocks I came to the right house. 20084. It was bright red with white trim. There was a porch light on, and other lights inside, upstairs and down. The sidewalk had a slick layer of ice on it now. I almost landed on my butt walking up to the front door. When I got there, I took one deep breath and rang the bell.

I heard thumping feet inside and a voice screaming, "I got it Mom! I got it! No problem!" When Henry opened that door a shot of yellow light fell out of that house and landed right at my feet on the front step, like it was trying to pull me inside.

"Alex! Alex Payne is here! My best friend! Hey Mom! Come and look!" Henry seriously jumped out that front door and grabbed me in this massive bear hug, and the funny thing was, I didn't pull away. In fact, all of a sudden there wasn't just snow on my cheeks any more. Big, fat tears were plopping out of my eyes right on to poor Henry's head. No sound was coming out of me, just those sorry drops coming down harder than the snow. I kept telling myself I was no crybaby, but I just couldn't stop.

Then a lady who I guessed was Henry's mom turned up at the door. "Who's this, Henry?" she asked, looking real confused.

"My best friend, Mom, Alex Payne. Can he come in for dinner? Please? Please?" All the while Henry was dragging me inside, like hanging out in there was a done deal. I didn't know what to do, so I went ahead and followed him. And Mrs. Rieder, she did this weird thing. Without even saying a word, she reached over Henry's head and wiped my cheek with the back of her hand, real gentle, like she was afraid she might hurt me somehow. I wanted to pull away, but Henry was dragging me right to her. So there was that hand, soft like a whisper, maybe trying to take some of my pain away.

"We got tuna noodle casserole right in here, Alex. That's my favorite, yes sir, and I bet you like it too, because you're my best friend. My best friend has to like tuna noodle casserole, and butterscotch pudding for dessert." And even though I *hate* tuna fish, I have to say that sounded like the best dinner a boy could have.

"Come on in, Alex," said Mrs. Rieder in this quiet voice, and she put her arm around my shoulder. "Alex's best friends are always welcome here. Just come on in."

PERFECT

When you're fourteen
And you're pretty
Your hair swinging down across your back
In a shimmering silver sheet
Your lip gloss shiny and fresh
All the time
Clothes brand new
Tight in the right places
And the wrong ones too
When your teeth are straight
Without braces
And your skin is pink
And clear
When your grades are A's
And the teachers worship you
Ask if you have siblings coming soon
When your locker is neat
Your notebooks organized
And you're always on time
When you receive 50 texts a day

And boys put anonymous love notes
In your locker
When you smile all the time
And giggle like a Disney princess
Eat lunch at the "best" table

Nobody asks
Why you always wear
Long sleeves
Nobody wonders if you

Margin Notes

Lie awake
Worrying about getting into
The right college
Wondering if your friends
Saw you chatting with
Leon, the nerd, after school
Hoping that you won't
Have to stay up until midnight
To get all your homework done
Tomorrow night

Everyone assumes
That you are content
Ditzy, stupid, unaware
Empty-headed

No one guesses that you are alone
That your mom and dad
Leave you to figure it all out
For yourself
Because you're the "good" kid
The "easy" kid
Not the older brother who screams
And hits his teachers
And wears diapers
And cannot form words
Locked inside himself
Your parents don't worry
About you
Because you're in Student Council
Honor Society
The star of the musical
On the Honor Roll again

When you're all these things
No one needs to know that
Your wrists are a maze

Of scars and scabs
That your best friends are
A paperclip and the metal tip
Of your mechanical pencil

When you're perfect
The truth is a curse

Moon Secrets

I hate it when my nail polish doesn't match my outfit. Once Ms. Metzler stopped a lecture on double negatives right in the middle of a sentence because she caught a whiff of my Ravishing Rojo. I said, "You must have eyes in the front of your head, Ms. M." This made her laugh, I'm not sure why, but it saved my neck. What's a girl to do? It's really tough to do your nails on a crowded school bus. In class, I can prop my feet up on the desk if I fold myself up just right. The point is, when my nails clash with my clothes, my day goes right down the toilet. I guess I'm kind of a perfectionist or something.

In fact, my sister Mae says I have a complex. Well if *I* have one and *she* doesn't I'm thinking maybe she should find one somewhere. She used to say, usually while she was pounding on me with some random piece of junk from our bedroom floor, that I was obsessed with everything being just so, and that I was uptight, and that no boy was ever going to want me.

Now just what am I supposed to say to that? Every morning at school there's a line of slobbering guys waiting at my locker. I find this pretty annoying, to be honest. They want to carry my books, or walk me to class, or buy me a slushy at lunch. One time Keagan Balch actually came up behind me and stroked my hair! Can you believe that? Way creepy! I whipped around and racked him with my purse as quick as Jackie Chan doing a karate chop. He didn't even have time to run away.

42

But what was I talking about? Oh yeah. Catching boys. And Mae. So here I am. My hair is pretty cool, I have to admit. It's really shiny, kind of like a waterfall of black ink, and I can always get it to style like a super model, on the FIRST TRY! Any time, any place. I guess I'm pretty lucky in the looks department. I know it, but I try not to make a big deal about it. I hate it when girls get all prissy and stuck up and start picking their friends because of makeup and clothes and junk like that. I just don't care. I pretty much will talk to anyone who talks to me. It makes life interesting, right?

But still, I'm pretty curvy for a thirteen year old, in all the places boys like to look when they think you're not paying attention, and sometimes when they know you are. My eyelashes are real long and thick too – no mascara for me. And to top it all off, I've never had a zit, at least not one the public could see. I had one on my right butt cheek once, like you really needed to know that, right? So I got the breaks in terms of the way I look. My mom says I look like her, which I guess is kind of true. She always smiles and plays with my hair when she says that. Then she says that Mae looks like my "waste of skin" long gone dad, and scowls. Nice, huh? Needless to say, Mae didn't get quite so lucky.

So all the boys chase after me, even though I think they're as dumb as dodos most of the time. It's amazing they don't go extinct! Sure, I like to flirt. I'm a pro at it; I watch a lot of reality TV. But I never get carried away. Why? Because I am headed for great things. I am going to graduate from high school, and then Harvard, and become a big-time CEO of a Fortune 500 company. (When I'm not watching TV, I read – a lot – about all kinds of stuff, including how to be a millionaire by the time you're 30.) I'm not going to have some loser boy sidetrack me – no way. That's what happened to Mom, and now Mae. Not me. Not a chance.

The boys don't chase after Mae, at least not the boys at school. But then Mae doesn't come to school so much these days, anyway. I never said this to her, but if she took care of herself a little better, she'd be really pretty. I didn't want her to get a big head or anything. Now I wish I'd told her something like that every single day. Maybe it would have made her stay. The last time I saw her, her hair was stringy-greasy, and she was so skinny. She kept looking down at her feet, or looking away. She wouldn't look at *me*. And she had this rash or something up and down her forearms. It looked like it really hurt, but when I asked her about it, she told me to mind my business. Then she left.

This was a couple of weeks ago, when she ran away again, that is. I'm pretty sure I know where she is. At night I feel like I can hear her whispering to me, and I'm pretty sure she's crying, but she's just a ghost in the room, and I can't help her. Mostly I just wake up and miss her. It's really empty and cold in the room when she's gone.

But I'm the little sister, not the mom. Mom is out with some guy most nights right now...Frank? Hank? I don't usually see her until the morning because she comes in late, and then she's in a super-crabby mood most of the time. I think Mae wants to come home, but she wants us to think she's all brave and crazy or something dumb like that. I think maybe she's lost, too. Maybe she doesn't know which bus to take to get back here. That nasty old apartment she's probably staying in is a ways from here. And I think she'll die soon. I just have a real heavy, dark feeling about it in my gut.

Mae swears she's just fine, but I know a secret. I know that she has a pretty scary feeling in her gut, too. Maybe a rumble, or a flutter, kind of like you get after you eat spicy Mexican food too fast. I saw the stick with the pink plus sign shoved under some tissues in our trash can the last time Mae was here. I wonder if that means it's going to be a girl? Mae doesn't know that I know, which is too bad, because I'm excited to be an auntie. On the other hand, Mae can't take care of herself, so what's she going to do with a tiny little baby? It's like a trashy talk show topic or something. I guess it probably doesn't matter, because babies take some time to grow inside, and some love, too, I think, and Mae won't be around for long. I'll miss her when she goes, and that little baby who I'll never meet. I'll miss that baby, too. I wonder if she even knows who the daddy is?

So how does a perfectionist like me end up with a sister like Mae? It starts in Viet Nam. I never lived there, but Mae did when she was real small. My mom and dad left with her in 1992, not because of a war or a crazy government or anything, just because they had no money. And in America, people had money to burn, or so they thought. They saved and begged and borrowed, and they got on a plane.

They ended up in Denver because a fourteenth-cousin-twice-removed or something like that had an extra room in his apartment. I was born a few years later. The cousin worked in a Pho restaurant on Federal, and he slept most of the day, so apparently we had to stay real quiet most of the time. I don't remember much, but Mae has told me about that apartment being dark, and smelling like old ladies and sweaty feet and kitchen grease. She remembers all kinds of banging, crashing, and yelling through the walls. And she remembers that all four of us lived in one bedroom, until my dad left, that is. My dad bussed tables at the restaurant for a few years, but one day he got on the bus after work and he just didn't come home. If anyone knows where he went, they never told me. I guess I might like to ask him someday, even though I barely remember him. I do know what made him go—that's a no-brainer. My mother is a witch.

I don't mean the pointy-hat black-cat kind of witch. I think I'd like that kind of witch better. My mom is just plain *evil*. What I can remember most about being a little kid is that Mom screamed at my dad all the time. She threw things, she hit him, she called him nasty names. And he never spoke or moved. He just sat there, usually with his head in his hands. I was three when he finally gave up. Mae was six.

As soon as my mom figured out he wasn't coming back, she started to hate my sister instead. Maybe it's because she did look a little like him, I don't know. Her words would fly out of her mouth in a big old mess of Hmong and English, and her tiny arms would windmill at Mae, sometimes hitting, sometimes not even coming close. I don't know a lot of Hmong to this day, but I sure know how to cuss in two languages. She was a loose cannon; you never knew what was going to freak her out. The weird thing is, I don't remember Mae ever being a bad girl back then. She played pretty quietly most of the time, and would always fix me a PBJ for dinner when Mom didn't come home. She brushed my hair, and sang to me when I was scared. To tell the truth, Mae was more my mommy than my mommy was when I was little. I don't think that was fair to her at all.

My mom went on hollering at Mae for years. She also spent a lot of time trying to "fix" Mae. In my mom's opinion, my sister was ugly, stupid, rude, disobedient, and a whole lot of other things that I sure never saw. Sometimes I think *all* my mom saw was my dad. I don't know that she even ever really met Mae.

My mom seems to think she's some kind of Vietnamese voodoo-magician-superwoman or something. I don't know where she gets all the garbage she comes up with. I'm just glad she never tried any of her whacked out spells on me. Poor Mae. When she was eight, mom brought home a big old jar of these slimy, snail-looking buggy things. They were wiggling around, trying to get out of the jar I think. I screamed and hid behind the living room curtains.

She sat Mae down on a stained, green towel on the living room floor. Like I said, Mae was a good girl. She really tried not to make my mom mad, so she did what she was told most of the time. Then, I can still see this in my mind because I couldn't believe it, Mom started to take those creepy-crawlies out of that jar and stick them all over Mae's bare arms. I screamed and then started to bawl, LOUD, but Mae just sat there. Little red dots of blood oozed out of her skin. It turns out the critters were leeches. Her hands trembled but she didn't make a single sound. My mom slapped her when she wet herself because she "messed up" that cruddy old towel.

My mom was babbling about how the leeches would pull all the bad poison out of Mae. The only time I can remember my mom smacking me was when I asked her, if Mae was full of bad poison, wouldn't she already be dead? Looking back at it, I'm pretty sure that's when Mae *started* to die, from the inside out. I wonder if that rash she has on her arms now reminds her of those leeches.

Then there was the time Mom took Mae to the back of that dry cleaner's over in Commerce City. As usual, I was there. I don't think Mom ever got us a babysitter. I was wearing a big white frilly dress with a yellow bow in front, because my mom had told me we were going somewhere special. I must have been about eight. Mae was wearing a yellow tank top with a purple stain on the right side, and a pair of dirty old cut offs. She didn't have a pretty dress, but maybe she knew where we were going, too.

It was shadowy in that back room. There were big, dead bugs lying on the floor in one corner. It smelled a little like pickles, and a little like something gone rotten. Like when Mae and I found the dead kitten in the alley behind our apartment, the one that had been hit by a car then cooked in the sun for a while. At the cleaner's, there was a long wooden table in the middle of the room with some dark brown splotches on it. I was just as horrified as Mae when my mother commanded her to take off her clothes and lie down on that table, right there in front of the old, wrinkly, dry-cleaning guy! As usual, I began to cry, but this time mostly because I figured I'd be next.

Mae just followed directions, knowing she'd get a beating if she didn't. She lay there on her back in her underwear, goose bumps popping up all over her arms and legs. She stared up at the ceiling while that nasty old man with the yellow teeth stuck needles into her arms and legs. He kept telling my mother all the while that Mae's "energy was very bad." He said he was going to set her straight. Mae ended up with 28 bruises (I counted them) all over, and my mom kept right on yelling at her. I know now that this crazy dude was pretending to do acupuncture, and that can really help some people if the person who's doing the poking is a professional. But this guy was a *dry cleaner*.

So I guess this didn't "fix" my sister. In fact, it was right about that time that she stopped taking showers on a regular basis. When she fixed food for me, she never ate anything. She started to go for really long walks late at night. She would come home when the sky was turning pink. I don't think she knew I heard her crying herself to sleep. She stopped getting up for school in the morning. Mom didn't even know she was still in bed.

But when Mom did run into Mae, she just wouldn't quit. It's like she saw all the bad stuff in the world in her, and didn't even bother to ask for any of the good. Like this: Mae was a poet. She used to write me these really pretty poems all the time and leave them in my book bag, or under my pillow. She wasn't really good at English, but somehow the words for the poems seemed to fall right out of her heart and dance around on the paper. And she made sure I got up for school, and held my hair back if I was sick, and made sure I had clean clothes every day. Maybe Mom thought that Mae being quiet was rude. I think she just gave up on talking somewhere along the way.

My mom's last "cure" for Mae came just last year. On her fifteenth birthday my mom tackled Mae to the floor for a birthday surprise. She kneeled on Mae's back, smashing her face into the damp, mildewy living room carpet. I could hear Mae struggling to breathe. Mom pulled up the back of her shirt. With her Zippo, she heated up the edge of this ancient shot glass with "Viva Las Vegas" painted on the side. The glass was hot enough that my mom had to hold it with a crusty old dishtowel so she wouldn't burn her hand.

She pressed the glass down, and held it on Mae's bare back. I counted. One…two…three…four…five. This time Mae screamed. She couldn't help it. I actually thought I heard a little sizzle, like drops of water in a frying pan, when the glass hit her skin. Mae kicked out at my mom, but for how tiny she is, my mom is tough. She held her ground. When she finally lifted the glass up, it held tight to Mae's skin, then let go with a "pop." It left a perfect round, red circle. Mom put that glass down six more times, for luck, she said, in different places on Mae's back. She muttered something about "sucking out the demons" but I'm the only one who heard her. Mae passed out after round one, which seems like it was lucky for her. She ran away for the first time that night.

She would come and go. Sometimes I would miss her, but mostly I just got on with my business. I did my homework, washed up the dishes, and went to bed early most nights. I didn't mess with any of Mae's stuff in our room. I figured she'd come back for good in the end. Besides, I didn't want to get her all mad at me.

But this time she hasn't come back home. Now she's hooked up with some big-time gang called the Shadow Warriors. I hear they're into all kinds of crazy stuff like stealing cars, doing drugs, and things like that. The last time I talked to Mae on the phone, it went something like this:

"When are you coming home, Mae?"

"Are you kidding? I'm *never* coming back. I got a new family now. They don't rag on me like Mom. They treat me with some respect."

"But Nancy's cousin was in the Warriors, and he's dead now. She said you have to get jumped in. I don't want them to do that to you. She said they beat you until you bleed, and you just have to lie there and take it, and then you have to tell them thank you for letting them do that to you! That's not right, Mae! You let them do all that to you?"

"No way. It's different for girls. Don't worry about me. I'm a grown up now. I can take care of myself."

"Well if it's so easy, maybe I should come and…"

"NO! No way! You will never, ever do that, do you understand me? You're too good for this. Too smart."

"But you just said…"

"Never mind what I said. This is not the way for you to live. No."

"Mae, I miss you…"

But then she had to go. She mumbled that she loved me. I haven't heard from her since.

As you can see, I'm not like my sister. I'm chatty, sometimes too much. People like me. They want to be with me because I'm cute and fun. I do okay in school, and I get along with all my teachers. I keep myself clean and neat. I guess I make my mother proud because to this day she's never tried to suck any demons out of me. But I wish she could be just a little bit proud of my sister.

Last time I saw Mae in person she looked real bad. We didn't talk; she was in line at the convenience store across the street from my school. The rash was all bumpy on her arms, like a bunch of ants had taken a walk and had a snack along the way. She was so skinny her cheekbones were sticking out, and she looked kind of like a skull mask for a Halloween costume. I think maybe she's really sick, and I'm scared. Aren't you supposed to get all fat and pink when you have a baby in you?

But I guess I'll keep on going to school and minding my business until Mae decides to come home. I'm saving up my lunch money to buy a blanket for that little baby. I saw this big, fluffy yellow and blue one all covered in teddy bears at some fancy store in the mall. I figure that baby is going to need a good blanket to snuggle down into. Maybe Mae can curl up under it too.

I don't think I have a complex like Mae used to say. What I've got is eyes in the front of my head, just like Ms. Metzler. I can see good enough to know that my mom pulled all of that bad stuff about Mae out of the big blue sky. Maybe I'm just a goofy thirteen-year-old girl, but I know what's right and what's wrong. And I know what I want more than anything in life, even more than a bottle of nail polish to match every one of my outfits, and that's to be someone else's daughter. I'm pretty sure Mae would want that too. We can talk about it if she comes home tonight. I'd like that.

MAD SKILLS

I clutch my deck more tightly than my books
Impatiently I push back shaggy hair
Exit the building, conscious of the looks
Of grown-up anger, I *do* see you stare

For me the day begins at half-past three
I Rock and Roll and try an Axle Stall
Pop Shove It then Air Walk, do you *see* me?
Nose Crook, now watch and learn, I rarely fall

Kick Flip, tell me now that you're not impressed
You must admit I'm good at this *one* thing
So what if you don't like the way I'm dressed?
Primo to Primo, on my board I'm king.

To master tricks is education, too
It's not my problem if it bothers you.

SKYSCRAPERS

I.

When I was four years old, the world exploded, and I became an undercover outcast.

On September 11, 2001, I was in preschool. My best friend's name was Ruthie Pierce. Her mom had just dropped me off after the morning session at the Happy Castle when I found my mom sitting cross-legged in front of the TV in our living room. She was covering her mouth with her hand. Her eyes were wide and she was shaking her head over and over again.

My name is Femi Hassan. I am thirteen years old, and I am a Muslim. Femi means "love" in Arabic. My sister's name is Tepi, which means "tempest"...I kind of think my parents got the names backwards based on our personalities. I tend to be the stormy one, she's the peaceful, gushy one. But oh well. I am a regular middle school kid with a regular family. I have braces, I listen to Fergie, and I believe in Allah. I believe that girls, and women, have rights to own their own homes and to control their own money, as my religion states. I am an 8th grade feminist. I believe that women are equal to men in every way. In the evening, when I remember, I kneel down, touch my forehead to the ground, and I turn to Mecca and pray, but I have a lot going on in my life. Sometimes I forget. This year I fasted during Ramadan with my parents even though they tell me I don't have to until I'm older, and even then they'll leave it up to me.

I was born and raised in the United States. I would like to travel to Mecca one of these days. It matters to me to know where my roots are, to understand what it's all about. I believe in Islam, but not blindly. I like to know what's what in the world.

I can speak and write in Arabic, but most of the time I choose English. It was really important to my mom that I know my dad's language, even though she was born in the U.S., and I actually think it's kind of cool. Not many kids my age in a standard public school can read and write from right to left. Plus I think Arabic is beautiful to look at, like a work of art, not just letters on a page

I do not cover my head with a hijab, but my grandma does. She lives with us, in an apartment in our basement. She's in her eighties, and she's a little senile. She tends to say exactly what's on her mind whether it's politically correct or not. Like one time we were in an elevator downtown and this really tough gangster-looking guy got on. His pants were hanging below his butt, and his boxers were sticking out, plain as day. Thank goodness those were pulled up, right? Anyhow, my grandma launched into this monologue about how dumb the guy looked and how he should dress better and have some respect for himself. All the while I was trying to wedge myself as far back in the corner as I could, praying that this guy wouldn't pull out a gun and shoot us both right there. Keep in mind, my grandma is five feet tall on her tippy toes and weighs about 90 pounds. But what happened? He shrugged, turned and said to her, "It's the fashion, ma'am," and got off when he hit his floor.

My grandma's mantra is "I'm an old lady, I can say whatever I want." One of these days it's going to get her in big trouble, I swear. But even though I sometimes disagree with her choice of words, I do not disagree with her choice of clothing. She lived her whole life in Egypt until my dad married my mom. She moved over here with them since Grandpa was long gone. She has some really awesome scarves, all different colors and patterns, not just plain black or white. Some of them even have silver and gold thread woven into them so she sparkles when she catches the light. My grandma is beautiful in a classy old-lady kind of way. She wears a veil not because she has to, but because custom suggests a physical barrier between women and men. It's a tradition, and she abides by it. It's her decision. Not every Muslim woman chooses to cover her head. That's the point, it's a choice; at least it is here in the U.S.

Here are some things that I bet you didn't know about Islam. Did you know that there are more than four million Muslims in the United States? And that tons of words in Romance languages are descended from Arabic? How about this: The first mosque in the United States was built in Cedar Rapids, Iowa in 1934 by a bunch of Lebanese immigrants. All the graves in its cemetery face Mecca. Yeah, it's true. Weird, huh? Also, there have been hundreds of doctors, philosophers, anthropologists, writers, artists, you name it, who have come from Islamic countries over the years.

But I still don't advertise that I am a Muslim, that I pray in a mosque, that my grandma wears a hijab. Ever since I was a preschooler, a lot of people have given Grandma really cold looks walking down the street. I know it's because of what she wears on her head. Because of the way she dresses, it is clear that she is a Muslim. And to many people, Muslim means enemy, and what they see when they see my grandma, is probably skyscrapers.

II.

I remember on the TV, I saw hundreds of sheets of paper fluttering in the sky like frantic birds released from their cages. Stations kept freezing on one picture that reporters started to call "The Falling Man." He looked like a tiny spider dangling from a thread, attached to a web. But in the end, there was nothing for him to cling on to, nothing at all.

Every summer since I can remember we've gone to Abiquiu, New Mexico. It's really beautiful, on a kind of desert highway north of Santa Fe. The mosque there is kind of a center for learning about Islam in the U.S. But what I like is the peace and quiet. No one judges you there for being who you are or believing what you believe. The buildings are all in a kind of compound, and all sorts of people come to visit. You don't have to be a Muslim, and a lot of the visitors aren't.

This makes me feel a little less nervous about believing in Islam in this country. I've met a lot of people who have come down to the center to learn about what Islam means, not because they want to convert or anything, but because they just don't know. And instead of assuming things about me because of my religion, they come to ask questions, to listen, and to open their minds. It's cool. Of course, it doesn't hurt that Georgia O'Keefe lived in Abiquiu for years and years and painted landscapes around here, especially the Pedernal Mountain. So sometimes tourists will come to visit her old house and stumble across the mosque. It's usually a pretty positive thing. The people who live and work and teach here are pretty open about who they are. Plus the rooms are comfy and the food is great!

I love going to Abiquiu. It makes me feel like I'm going home, even though it's a few hundred miles south of *home* home in Boulder. I love watching the chili roasters on the side of the road, seeing the willows along the Rio Grande change color, watching the sunset over the Jemez Caldera like it's actually a volcano about to erupt. It's beautiful, scary, desolate country, a little like being on another planet, I think. And a lot of the time in the car there is no noise except for the wind and whatever water the river's holding at that particular time. And my sister texting, of course.

It seems kind of strange though; you don't have to have a place to "get away" and find yourself as a Christian. But being Muslim in the U.S. means being separate, even though the Koran talks all about social equality. I don't think it much matters what we do, we'll never be considered a part of the mainstream society, you know? People seem to think that we don't believe in God, and that we're all on some holy mission to destroy everyone in America. That makes no sense. I *am* American. Why would I be out to wreck the world I live in? I believe in *Sunna*, the right way, and it does not include hurting people because they don't believe the same things as you. No way.

Still, only my very best friends and a couple of my teachers at school know that I am Muslim. It's all hush-hush, like I have some kind of fatal disease or something. To be fair, the secrecy is my choice. I have red hair, freckles, and green eyes. I get all that from my mom. As my dorky sister said to me once, "Relax, *you* don't look like a terrorist." What's that supposed to mean? What does a terrorist look like? But she's right, I guess. I don't look like the guys we've been hunting in Afghanistan and Iraq for as long as I can remember. But that's the problem right there. People might assume stuff about me if they know

I'm a Muslim. I don't mind people being curious and asking questions, I just don't appreciate being judged for one piece of who I am.

When I was fasting last November, a ridiculous rumor started. Middle school is *all* about rumors, right? Unfortunately, yes. I'm pretty popular at my school. I have a lot of friends and acquaintances and I get along with pretty much everyone. Our lunch table is usually pretty crowded. So when I wasn't eating, John O'Brien made a stupid joke about me being anorexic. I had to look the word up in a dictionary, for crying out loud. But wouldn't you know it, by the end of the day there was a text marathon going on about how I was dying because I was starving myself and was getting checked into hospital that very night. I didn't want to deal with the drama, so I broke my fast. I sat down at the table the next day, told John that maybe he could stand to skip the bag of Doritos he was inhaling, and proceeded to eat my sandwich. Case closed. But it bugs me that I can't do something that is important to me without having to explain it to the world. It's nobody's business but my own.

III.
Then there was a deep, steady rumble, like a train bearing down, too fast too close, and the first tower collapsed as though the ground had opened up and swallowed it whole.

My dad is Egyptian, and the reason I am Muslim. My mom is actually a Colorado native. She traveled to Cairo to attend the American University for graduate school. She met my dad at some fancy party with lots of college professors and business people. My dad was, and is, an oilman. He was working in Hurghada, a seriously swanky resort town on the coast of the Red Sea. He knew a few of the professors, and was in town, so he just happened to drop in for a cocktail. The rest is history. He fell for my mom's wit, independence, and curves, he says. Gross! However, that is the reason I'm here. My mom *is* really smart. She was working on a degree in linguistics with a minor in Arabic. She's actually a librarian at C.U. in Boulder. She speaks and reads English, French, Spanish, and Arabic fluently, so she's kind of a hot commodity.

Anyhow, when my parents hooked up, my dad made it really clear that he didn't care if my mom was Muslim or not, even though he is. To be honest, he doesn't do a whole lot of praying. He spends more time online and in conference calls for work. But he does still call himself faithful, and he still believes in the Koran, he just has other priorities, too. So my parents lived together in Cairo for about a year, then decided to move to the U.S. There were oil opportunities in Colorado, and that's where my mom is from, so they headed back. They arrived with my grandma in tow and had a huge, traditional Western wedding with the white frilly dress and the huge cake and all that crazy stuff. The ceremony was all in English. (Every now and then, if my parents are arguing about some dumb little thing, my dad will threaten that he can technically go off and get three other wives if she doesn't quit telling him to mow the lawn. Of course he would never really consider such a thing. He thinks he's really funny.) My dad was kind of old, forty or so, when all this took place. They said, "I do" and bought a house on Mapleton Hill in Boulder. I hear that my grandma was not too jazzed about Dad marrying my mom, but they learned to get along. In fact, they actually seem to enjoy each other's company these days, as far as I can tell.

My dad has a brother in Cairo, so he and my mom and my grandma have gone back every few years since they moved to the U.S. When I was ten, they took me and my older sister to visit for the first time. It was amazing. To give you some perspective, Egypt is about as big as Texas and California combined. There are on average only five or so days of rain per year, and it is crazy hot. We went in December, on our winter break, and it was as hot as Colorado in August. No kidding. Amazingly, there are still trees everywhere: acacia, carob, date palm, eucalyptus, and because the Nile is right there, you get the sense is that it's actually a kind of "green" place, but that's just an illusion. Just a few miles out, the whole country becomes this totally unforgiving desert. It's crazy.

Cairo is about 100 miles from the coast and oozing with about 18 million people. It is a huge, crazy, crowded, polluted city. Apparently there aren't enough jobs at all for how many people live there, so there are a lot of people begging and living on the streets. The pollution in the air has killed a lot of trees, and is actually eroding monuments.

Scary to think that that same toxic stuff is touching your skin every time you walk outside.

On the other hand, Cairo is a really spectacular place. There are street bazaars every day and they are literally a rainbow of people and cultures. There are multicolored fabrics and clothes for sale everywhere, delicious schwarma and falafel steaming on carts, jingly music that makes your toes tap, and lots and lots of people noise. But one of the things I noticed right away was the lack of females. There are hardly any women wandering the market places, unless they're tourists, and the few who are out and about usually have their heads and arms covered. It's a pretty conservative place, I guess. There are tons of sidewalk cafes but they are filled with men, drinking that strong, smelly coffee, and smoking. I swear, everybody smokes. Talk about culture shock!

But then there's the whole out-doorsy bit. There is this awesome place called the Ras Muhammad National Park on the tip of the Sinai Peninsula. It has amazing coral reefs, hundreds of different kinds and colors of fish, all of which look somehow electrified, and tons of different types of birds…osprey and herons all over the place. I found out after we visited that this was actually where my dad proposed to my mom! Kind of takes the fun out of the visit for me, but oh well! Egypt just has these really cool natural places to visit, and the government is finally trying to do something about not letting them get destroyed. Seems like common sense to me.

So we stayed with my uncle Nizan and his wife and kids in his apartment in a high-rise in the middle of Cairo. The place was full of ghastly furniture, really fancy and detailed, with lots of curlicues and gold and stuff all over it. It looked like stuff you would see in a museum, or maybe a flea market, but apparently that's how you show your wealth in that part of the world. They also have a maid who waits on the family hand and foot, even though Nizan's a clerk in an electronics shop and my aunt stays home all day. Apparently it's a status thing. I find it all to be completely hideous.

While we were there, Nizan took us to the Muhammad Ali Mosque, and no, it doesn't have any relation to the boxer. That's what I assumed, too. But it is truly, absolutely, seriously phenomenal. It has five gigantic white domes, and these turret things that look like rocket ships shooting off the roof. They're called minarets. I don't know what exactly the inside is made of, but it literally *glows* like the walls are solid gold. And it has a huge courtyard with all these complicated carvings on the archways, and a beautiful clock tower as well.

It was pretty impressive, I have to admit. But not as impressive as the pyramids. We traveled to Giza to see them, and boy did I feel small. And young, And insignificant. It puts all the little worries and troubles in your life into perspective, you know? I can't even imagine trying to move a single one of the stones that make up those monuments. That is definitely a feeling I will not forget. Standing there, for just a second, I got it. This was a culture 6000 or more years old, and I was *ten*. I knew all of a sudden that I was a little tiny piece of an enormous puzzle. The puzzle needed me to be complete, but it wouldn't fall apart without me, either. Now that's a scary concept.

We did some other touristy stuff too. We went to a puppet show where the puppets were held up on sticks behind a white screen with light projected through it and all you saw were their shadows. I guess this is very traditional, but I found it pretty creepy! We took a ride in a felucca, which is a type of sailboat, down the Nile. At one point my dad crept up behind me and gave me a shove, yelling, "Watch out for crocodiles!" Not funny, not funny at all. I almost peed my pants I was so scared. We also got to witness the sport of sports for Egyptians: soccer. We watched the Al Ahly club cream their opponents. I have never seen people so fired up about a game! Holy crud! It was a pretty cool vacation overall.

And we ate *a lot*. Don't get me wrong, we eat really great food at home, but in Egypt we ate *all the time*. It's like my aunt Ebe thought we were *starving* or something. I think this was partly a show for company, but I'm not kidding, we ate *5 times a day!* Saffron rice, fresh, juicy dates and watermelon, stuffed grape leaves, lentils, babaghannooj, home made bread, you name it, we ate it. The smell of onions and lemons and roasting lamb became pretty much permanently stuck in my nose. Not that that's a bad thing. The food was *delicious*; we were just *stuffed* all the time! I love Egypt. I love my heritage. But my home is a world away.

V.

I could almost smell the smoke as it billowed in black waves from the top of those two skyscrapers, through ragged gashes in the steel. I squeezed into the nest formed by my mom's crossed legs…warm, safe.

Slowly but surely it became clear to me that there's more to me than my religion. That's just one part of my culture, of who I am, of who my family is. I am from a river that flows North, and the sun melting away over the Pharoahs like liquid fire. But I am also from haj and *Masha ' Allah*. And I am also from Hannah Montana and Pikes Peak. Do you see what I mean? I am from the sky, and the earth, and the water and the air. I am from the family I love, and the ancestors I've never met. It's not enough to say that I am Muslim. Not by a long shot. I am a kaleidoscope, and if people can't see that every time my colors shift I am beautiful, maybe they should look away.

VI.

I could feel the tremors in my mom's hands as she watched. I clasped them tightly and rubbed them between mine, looking for comfort in the familiar, rough creases, but they were shaking, and I was afraid.

When the second tower came down, my mom said that everything was about to change, and she was right. While we had always been viewed as a little different by neighbors and friends, we had never been totally pointed out and ignored. Ostracized, my mom calls it. I can still remember for about a month after 9/11 people would sometimes actually cross the street to get away from us if we were with my grandma. One day when we were at a 7-11, my mom was obliviously pumping gas into our Volvo. I was in the back seat reading *Yertle the Turtle*. Grandma was in the front passenger seat. The windows were down. Some guy came right up to my grandma and started cussing at her, saying "How dare you side with *them*," and that she was "un-American," then he spat *into the car*. This is one of the most vivid memories I have of childhood. I also remember him glancing at me through the window and muttering something about how murderers shouldn't be allowed to live in this country. I was crying at this point, and my grandma was out of the car, swinging at the guy. And my mom, the gentle, eloquent, composed librarian was throwing profanities at this stranger who dared to scare her baby. He finally went back to his own car, assaulting us with random insults the whole way.

So Mom was absolutely right. Everything had changed. I went from being a "regular" kid to being a target because people were making assumptions about my family. The kids at my school didn't really bother me. It's hard to process that kind of stuff when you're in preschool. But I did get a few comments that kids had probably overheard from their parents. A couple of my friends were suddenly not allowed to come over and play. It was really quiet in our house for a few weeks. My mom and dad actually started talking about home-schooling us, or taking out a second mortgage to pay for a private school. They were seriously scared about our being hurt or harassed. After the fact, Tepi, who is three years older than me, told me that she had been teased a lot at school. She looks a lot more like my dad than my mom, black hair, nearly black eyes, dark skin, so combine that with her name, and she became a victim. Tepi has never stood up for herself the way I do. She's not a fighter. Her feelings get hurt really easily, and she's naturally shy. So when kids started calling her horrible names and telling her she didn't have a right to still be alive, well seriously, how does a seven year old deal with that? She came home sobbing for nights in a row. My parents didn't know what to do. Some days they kept her home. They talked to the teachers and the principal, but the kids were doing this in the halls, on the playground, out of earshot of adults. That's the way it usually happens. In the background, my grandma was unusually quiet.

But after a while, it stopped. It's like there was an electric charge running through the world in the aftermath of the collapse, and finally, the battery went dead. Even now, people still give my grandma funny looks sometimes. She says she likes to give people something to think about. But sometimes I think people just speak and act out of fear rather than thinking from their hearts. We're just people, after all.

My grandma, shopping for groceries at Earth Style in her rainbow-striped scarf, is just a person, but so were all the people who died on September 11, including the eight little kids, younger than me, who were vaporized inside three commercial airplanes. I'm just a person, too, and this world scares me a lot.

I think that when the world falls apart in a matter of hours, when people realize that they can't keep their families safe no matter how much they might want to, when airplanes tumble out of the sky and skyscrapers explode, I think we *implode*. I think we stop thinking like human beings and start cowering like frightened animals. I think we lash out at each other because we are terrified that anything, anyone different than us must be a threat. And when we curl up into those little balls, wishing we were little babies again, we can't see what's going on around us. And then we die inside.

When I was four years old, I learned the meaning of fear. When the sky fell, I knew my world would never be completely safe again, for me or anyone else. But the hardest thing is knowing that there are people in the world who will always be afraid...of me.

COOPERATIVE LEARNING

All Monty McGee really wanted was a pencil. He came into class that morning with a smile on his warm, brown face. Miraculously, he had made it into the building on time, even though he'd snored through two snooze cycles. On the way to school, he had shoveled two frosted strawberry toaster tarts into his mouth in quick succession so his stomach wouldn't start rumbling until at least second period. Kayleigh, the cute girl with the long dark hair and the indigo eyes, had flipped her hair at Monty and smiled before turning back to giggle with her friends at her locker before first period. And on this day, the fact that Monty was taller than all the other boys in sixth grade, and that his voice had changed, and that his green eyes pierced the room incongruously within that warm, latte face, none of these factors seemed to matter. All was right with the world. Monty was full, relaxed, and ready to face the day.

But all this changed the moment he sat down in Mr. King's social studies class. Monty was actually pretty psyched to be there that fateful Wednesday morning. The topic of discussion for the past week or so had been the Aztecs. Finally, some blood and guts! Monty was really looking forward to another day of Web exploration in the realm of human sacrifice, torture, bizarre bodily mutilation, and general carnage. Now *that* was what education should be all about, at least to Monty's way of thinking. But sadly, there would be no surfing on this day. Instead, Mr. King barked five words that dropped all Monty's morning giddiness into a dark, crusty pit in the bottom of his stomach, a chasm so deep and treacherous that there was no hope of retrieving that sorry little ray of sunshine from its echoing depths.

"Everybody get out a pencil!"

The command reverberated within Monty's brain like a death sentence. Organization was not Monty's strong suit. At his house, this was a given. Monty's mom, a red-headed, emerald-eyed, creamy-skinned *Amazon* of an Irish woman, spent a good number of her waking moments harping on him to get his stuff together. Clean the room, (this did not involve, much to Monty's dismay, shoving everything under the bed,) put the dirty clothes in the hamper, do your homework, put the homework in the backpack, *make sure you have the supplies you need for tomorrow*. Monty's dad, of similar stature to his mom, but with skin as dark as polished mahogany, reinforced these expectations by threatening to remove basketball privileges from Monty's life indefinitely if he didn't get it together. This was a daily routine that met with debatable success. Organization was not Monty's number one priority on this brilliantly sunny, potentially stress-free Wednesday morning in March. And it was time to find a pencil.

Monty began to search. He dug around in the pockets of his baggy jeans, the ones too short by two inches for his rapidly stretching legs. Alas, all he uncovered was a green rubber band, an unwrapped, fossilized Tootsie Roll of dubious origins, and a filthy scrap of paper bearing the directions to the basketball court near his buddy Mario's house. No luck. So he moved on to the notorious binder. Monty kept all of his papers for all of his classes carefully stashed inside an orange plastic folder resembling an accordion. This made perfect sense to Monty. If all his papers were in one place, it was harder to lose them. Never mind the fact that within this black hole existed a conglomeration of unfinished items so varied and chaotic that even if Monty hired a personal assistant, the results would be limited in effect. Not surprisingly, there was no pencil in the bottom of this pit. In fact, the only "writing utensil" to speak of was half of a broken purple crayon retrieved from the grasp of Monty's baby brother at the breakfast table, shortly after said sibling had spat it out of his mouth.

Pencil? No. Monty released a deep, troubled, and plainly audible sigh, and started to consider Plan B.

Unfortunately, in his happy-go-lucky frame of mind that day, Monty hadn't considered the need for a backup plan in order to achieve academic success. It was time to think fast, and think smart, as his dad would say. Monty decided in that split second to do the logical thing: Ask for a pencil.

"Mr. K., I don't have a pencil."

"That's not my problem, Monty." The finality and meaning of this statement was clear to most of the people in the room, except for Monty. He was a resourceful individual, and had been taught from a young age to never give up. He had also learned early on, that in his gigantic, eclectic, eccentric family, you looked to each other for guidance and support in times of need. Take the time that Monty rode his bike into the creek behind his house when he swerved off the trail to avoid a pack of Boy Scouts on a nature walk. As he hollered and gurgled and thrashed about in the murky shallows, who should come chattering along but his Auntie Fay and her boyfriend Marco! As they fished Monty out of the muck, still clinging to his precious bike, Fay asked Monty what in heaven's name he would have done if they hadn't happened along.

"Someone I was related to was bound to come by eventually," Monty surmised. Fay couldn't really argue, as half the neighborhood seemed to be populated with McGees in one form or another. Block parties tended to resemble family reunions, and everybody knew everybody else's business, no matter how insignificant it might seem.

So when faced with the question of how to proceed without a pencil, Monty didn't hesitate. He didn't have one of his own, so he politely, quietly, reservedly leaned over and asked his neighbor, Kevin. Kevin shrugged off the request. He could barely take care of his own academic needs, let alone focus on somebody else's plight. So Monty turned the other way, and in a similarly hushed manner asked Stacey. Stacey only had a hot pink gel-pen, and the request from the dashing Monty caused her to burst into a fit of hiccupy giggles. This caught the attention of Molly, Abby, and Jenni with an "i", all of whom began to whisper to each other, though separated by two rows of desks apiece, about how Monty clearly liked Stacey. Still no pencil.

Mr. King cleared his throat loudly and shot "the look" at nobody in particular and everyone at once, the look that could turn a raging grizzly into Winnie the Pooh. The class grew silent.

Monty, however, remained oblivious to these goings-on. His objective was clear. He needed a writing utensil, and fast. It was apparently time for Plan C: If all else fails, ask the teacher again.

"Mr. K., I asked everybody, and no one has a pencil they can loan me. Do you have one?"

"I already told you no, Mr. McGee. It's your responsibility to come to class prepared. Figure it out."

To tell the truth, Monty was a little puzzled at this suggestion. He was trying to be polite, trying really hard not to be disruptive, but he was running out of options. More than anything at that moment Monty wanted to hop online and learn a new form of human sacrifice, or maybe some excellent form of body-piercing practiced in Meso-America. But apparently this was not to be, and his fate today revolved around the acquisition of the coveted 2B. On to Plan D.

He started by doing a quick scan of the room. No luck. There were no pens or pencils near enough to Monty's desk for him to roll one over inconspicuously with his size thirteen shoes. So quietly, calmly, slowly, like a giraffe getting up from a picnic with a herd of Shetland ponies, Monty slid out of his seat and made his way to the back of the room to "Get a Kleenex." Once there, Monty waited for Mr. King to turn his back to the class then dropped with all the stealth he could muster to all-fours and shot like a human torpedo into the corner of the room. He glanced frantically back and forth in that quadrant. No pencil. As Mr. King turned from the lecture notes on the board, Monty threw himself behind Luci Sharp's desk. Luci muttered something rude and unnecessary under her breath but didn't rat him out. When Mr. King turned to face the board again, Monty scurried into quadrant two. This time he found a yellow colored pencil and a stick of spearmint gum, still in its wrapper. He also noticed that Casey Swanson had a birthmark shaped like Texas on her right ankle, and that Justin Green had recently farted. Still no pencil.

Pocketing the yellow implement and the gum, Monty made one last break for it. As Mr. King shuffled over to his desk to acquire an eraser, Monty dove for quadrant three. He had been playing baseball for as long as he could remember, and could slide like a pro. Unfortunately, this time his athleticism did not serve him well. He overshot the spot he had been aiming for behind the TV cart and smashed into the front wall hard enough to make the white board shudder ominously. To add insult to injury, a cascade of dry-erase markers paused dramatically for a split second before pummeling Monty's head in quick succession. And the irony of it all was that now, wedged under his butt, was a brand new, unchewed, mechanical pencil, complete with an intact eraser. His salvation, but a moment too late. With a heavy sigh, Monty began to gather up the markers and place them carefully into the tray of the board. All the while, Mr. King, who had finally noticed Monty, was assaulting him with a barrage of choice comments about his ineptitude as a student, his clumsiness, his hopeless lack of tact, his clearly substandard I.Q., and his general worthlessness as a human being.

Monty sat there, defenseless and beaten, unable to come up with a reasonable response. Besides, that was how he'd been taught to behave. His family might not resemble the Brady Bunch, but rules were rules. Monty had been indoctrinated from an early age to respect his elders. This meant that when mom or dad or a teacher or some random adult on the street had something to say to you, you were to stand there and take it, because you were the child. The subordinate. The lowly one. The one without rights, privileges, or individual identity. Moreover, you were a representative of your family, and to show disrespect was to sully the good name McGee. This type of behavior was intolerable to Monty's parents, and the few times in his life that he had strayed from this mandate, he had regretted it deeply from the dismal confines of his technology-free bedroom.

So as Mr. King pounded Monty with verbal low-blows, he took it like a man. What Mr. King, mom, dad, and his classmates did not know was that even though Monty was taller, stronger, more popular, more confident than most kids his age, those vicious words made him shrivel up inside like a raisin that's slipped down the crack of the sofa cushions and been fossilized for a few months. The words crumpled him the way Monty had crushed and trashed the last test Mr. King had returned to him with a lurid red F emblazoned across the entire front page. The whole sticks and stones saying? Absolutely, 100% false.

Monty was destroyed profoundly and systematically under Mr. King's practiced syllabic assault.

Ultimately, of course, the result of the incident was for Monty to be removed from the classroom and sent to sit in the hall. There he was instructed to ponder the error of his ways, and as punishment, to write down the reason for his lack of preparedness for class. But he still did not have a pencil. So there Monty sat for 45 minutes, losing track of the initial reason for the conflict after about 45 seconds. He knew, based on past experience, that Mr. King would not bother to call his parents or send him to the office. There was simply something about Monty that pushed all Mr. King's buttons simultaneously, and ejecting Monty from the room was apparently the solution of choice. When other adults passed Monty in the hall, they shook their heads, rolled their eyes. One 6th grader actually scurried to the opposite side of the hall and sped up as if Monty was a predatory troll or something similar.

Class was almost over. Monty started to gather up his gangly limbs in preparation for a more successful attempt at his next subject. His feet got caught on each other during the ascent, and as he grabbed for the wall to save himself, he heard a high, bubbly laugh.

"Monty, what are you *doing* out here?"

Mrs. Kim had been Monty's art teacher the semester before. She wore eclectic color combinations on swirling patchwork skirts and pinned her silver hair back with paint brushes and chopsticks. She played didgeridoo and traditional Andean music during class. She allowed the kids to hum and tap and laugh while they worked. She encouraged them to respond to each other's creations. Mrs. Kim read poetry from the Harlem Renaissance and asked her students to paint what they heard. She sprayed the room in muck every time she lost focus on her potter's wheel. Even though she was ancient, probably 40, Mrs. Kim had a little diamond stud in her nose. She often came and sat at the art tables with the kids and worked *with* them. She said that the kids inspired her to be more creative and to take more risks. Mrs. Kim was *cool*. *Weird* but *cool*.

And never, not even once, had Mrs. Kim beaten a student down with words, as far as Monty could remember. She laughed a lot, smiled a lot, pulled kids quietly aside if they were screwing up. Sure, she had a look, and a good one at that. One that made you shake in your shoes like Medusa has caught you staring in her direction. But Mrs. Kim never yelled or made sarcastic comments. If she was really exasperated she might let out a heavy sigh, but she *never* made kids feel small.

So here she was, sauntering up to Monty as he regained his balance against the dirty grey brick of room 209, and she was grinning from ear to ear.

"Monty, I'm so glad to see you!" she beamed, and before Monty could reply, she was smothering him in a spectacular bear hug that did not match her diminutive form.

Monty couldn't help but let out a hint of a smile as he asked, "Ummm…why?"

"What do you mean why?" Mrs. Kim countered, clearly startled by the question. "I hardly ever get to see you any more! Aren't I allowed to miss one of my star students?"

Star student? Monty instinctively turned around to see the person to whom Mrs. Kim was referring, but it wasn't passing period yet. The hall was empty and echoing with her words. Monty wracked his brain. He wasn't *terrible* at art, but nor was he a prodigy. Star student? How could that be? He had made a pot that vaguely resembled a frog last October, and he had painted a self-portrait that Mrs. Kim said was Picasso-esque (that wasn't intentional, but he took it as a compliment) but *star student*? Come on now.

While Monty was pondering this, Mrs. Kim released him from her grip, stepped back, and just *beamed* at him. "I do so miss your presence in my class every day! There aren't many kids who can just brighten your world when they walk in a room, you know that?"

Slowly, Monty began to put the pieces together. According to Mrs. Kim, star student wasn't just about books and answers. It wasn't just about having a writing utensil. It was about being a positive part of a community, someone who adds a little sparkle to the room. This was revolutionary. Monty was silent now not on account of shame as he had been an hour before, but on account of this awesome revelation. Could there be more to school than worksheets and tests and rules? For the love of Pete, why hadn't anyone told Monty this before?

Meanwhile, Mrs. Kim had been chattering away to Monty about art shows and music and what she had eaten for lunch. Monty started frantically nodding his head in an attempt to prove that he had been thoroughly engaged in the conversation as an equal partner from the get go. He couldn't help grinning as he caught the thread of what she was saying. Suddenly, his presence in this building was validated somehow, and he was not afraid to advertise the fact.

At that moment the electronic tone to signal passing time echoed through the hallway. A veritable flood of students poured out of every door, including Mr. King's. That particular exodus was followed by a muttering and grumbling Mr. King, glaring at the mass of humanity blocking his own escape. When Mr. King finally made his way out of the room, Mrs. Kim greeted him as if psychically channeling Monty's discomfort at being confronted with his nemesis. Godzilla versus Spongebob, or something along those lines.

"Mr. King! How *are* you today? Do you know Monty? He is one of the most *wonderful* human beings on the planet. Don't you just adore a student who genuinely cares about the world around him? And about the well being of his classmates? Young people like Monty are hard to come by these days, aren't they? You're so lucky to have him! Well, have a fabulous day you two." She wandered off mumbling something about promises to keep, and pots to throw before she sleeps. Bizarre. All of this tumbled out of Mrs. Kim's mouth in the space of about seven seconds. Mr. King and Monty actually shared a moment of communal awe, perhaps the only time that they would see eye to eye in the entire course of their relationship. Their jaws dropped slowly, simultaneously as Mrs. Kim's animated monologue drew to a close. Then she was away, in a whirlwind of magenta and crimson. She didn't dematerialize like a fairy godmother, but Monty could almost see a trail of glittery dust trailing in her wake, a haze of positive energy bustling away down the hall, humming some jaunty, nameless tune.

Mr. King turned on his heel to face Monty, looked him up and down distastefully, as though noticing graffiti on a pristine white wall, gave a loud, dissatisfied "harrumph" and stormed off down the hall.

But for once, this disdain did not phase Monty. On the contrary, he couldn't stop smiling. He noticed Mario flirting with Kayleigh's friend, Devin, in front of the trophy case and made a spur of the moment decision. Drawing in a deep, cleansing, King-free breath, Monty shyly sidled up to Kayleigh and tapped her on the shoulder.

"Hey Kayleigh, can I borrow a pencil please?"

"Geez Monty. What took you so long to ask? I've got about a hundred of them. No big deal."

"Yeah, no big deal," Monty replied softly. But still, he could hear Mr. King and Mrs. Kim doing battle in his head, trying to create and destroy him in a twisted tango of wills. No big deal, or maybe the biggest deal of all.

AMULET

Dear Mama –

I am afraid that you are dead and gone, but even still, I'm writing to you to tell you that I'm ok. I wish you could know a lot of things about me, and there are so many things I wish I could ask you. But I know in my heart that I will never meet you. So I carry you inside of me and I try to believe that everything has worked out for the best.

Here is what I *do* know. I was born some time in 1996. No one seems to be able to figure exactly what the date was, so Mom and Dad called it March 6. Soweto is where they found me. I know this is a part of South Africa. They've described it for me and shown me pictures, and I've done some online research myself. I've read plenty about Apartheid and Nelson Mandela and even the Boer War. The book history is easy to find, but the history of me isn't so clear. My parents went to Soweto with their church in 1995 to help build houses out of cinder blocks and corrugated metal. They had seen pictures on TV of skinny little kids living in shacks made out of cardboard with black water running down dirt streets. So they went on a "mission" and tried to help. And they did help, a little. They built some houses, but for every one they put together they saw 100 more that were falling down. Mom and Dad tell me it was a sorry place full of pain and misery.

They met you there one day, carrying some water in a tin bucket from a community pump. You were *really* pregnant they said. You were exhausted and sick with AIDS, but your smile shot straight into their hearts. You told them all about the dreams you had for your child to grow up some place where education was a right for everybody, where girls didn't have to be afraid to walk down the street just because they weren't boys, where a disease like AIDS was treated with medicine, and where people weren't left to fend for themselves and to die. You explained to them that my father was a rich man you had worked for, cleaning his house. He had many children, and wanted none of them. My parents listened to you. My mom says that when they went back to the hotel that night, she cried and cried.

You stayed in touch with them for the rest of the time before I was born. My parents brought you food and tried to get you the medicine you needed. But they say they ran into a lot of something called "bureaucratic red tape." It seems to me that politics get in the way of doing the right thing way too much of the time on *both* continents! The night I was born my mom was beside you in the clinic. She says there were maybe 20 other women in one room all having their babies at just about the same time. The doctors and nurses were running all over trying to help everybody at once, cradling slimy babies, cutting cords, mopping up blood. She says she'd like to never hear that much screaming in one place again.

It took eighteen hours for me to arrive. In the end, a doctor from Scotland yanked me right out. Apparently I screamed as loud as most of the ladies in the room. You named me Naledi, an African word for "star." My mom says you held me for a few minutes, then handed me to her. She says you cried and cried, but real quietly, just tears, no sound. You told her you knew you were too sick to take care of me.

I don't know all the details of what happened next, but I know my mom and dad spent a lot of time talking to diplomats and agencies and government people. They signed lots of papers, made lots of promises, and gave people lots of money, my dad says, all so they could take me home with them. And in the end, in June of 1996, they did. They bundled me up in pink, fuzzy, American clothes and took me on the plane, first to Germany, then to New York, then on to Denver, Colorado. They say you wailed when you handed me over, but you also thanked them again and again. My mom says you didn't want to let me go, but in your heart, you felt it was the right thing to do for me.

I became Naledi Murphy. My parents have shown me all the adoption papers, and they show your name as Miriam Medupe. So I guess my name started out as Medupe, too. My parents are ok with me sending this letter to the adoption organization to try and reach you, but they're a little sad. They have warned me that you probably died of AIDS a long time ago. I know that thousands of people die in South Africa every year from AIDS, and that many little kids end up orphans because of it. But I just want to know if you're out there. And even if you are gone, I need to try. I need to speak my piece just in case you might hear.

My parents tell me I'm a lucky one because I got medicine pumped into me when you were pregnant and after I was born to keep me from getting sick. Not all kids have that kind of a chance. They tell me you all sent letters back and forth for a couple of years, but then the letters ran out. So they're pretty sure you didn't survive the disease. They say there isn't nearly enough medicine for the grown ups who are sick over there. I hope it's not true. I want you to be alive. I want you to know that I have all the things you wanted for me.

I've had kind of a funny life here so far. I'm twelve now. I'm a medium kind of height, and I have a long, ovally face that my mom says makes me look like royalty somehow. Once a month my mom takes me to a braiding salon in the middle of Denver. It's a pretty gross part of town, all dirty streets, run-down buildings, but Deena, the woman who braids my hair, is awesome. It takes *hours*. I sit and read or watch cartoons while Deena chatters away about who knows what. My mom usually goes to run errands while I'm sitting there. Sometimes it itches and pulls, but it looks really beautiful when it's finished. I know it's expensive for Mom and Dad, but they want me to feel "African." I don't know that having my hair braided makes me feel like I know where I come from, but I do like the way it makes me look.

I don't know if I should feel guilty about this, but I do *not* feel like

I am African. My mom tells me that I am the definition of African American, and that I should be proud of that. I know that's true. But I have never really seen Africa, only pictures online and in books. These braids in my hair are pretty, and the kids at school compliment me a lot, but the way I look does not make me who I am. I belong here, not on another continent. This is my home. I am American, but I feel kind of badly that I don't miss Africa somehow. I hope you can understand that. I'm having a little trouble with the idea, myself.

But this is my home. I live in a neighborhood and go to a school that is mostly made up of white kids. Sometimes this is weird for me. I feel like I stand out because I have this deep, dark brown skin, kind of like the color of the chestnuts on the tree in our backyard. One of the few other black kids at school is a friend of mine, and you wouldn't know she was black to look at her. She is kind of a sandy color, like a nice tan. Me, I stick out. Some days that's a good thing, like when my counselor said I reminded her of autumn fire on a snowy day. I've thought about that a lot. At first, I was a little embarrassed. She said that to me *at lunch* in front of *all my friends*. We all giggled, and I turned red. But then one of my friends said to her, "So what do I remind you of?" and she just said, "Hmmm…let me think about that." I'm ok with being autumn fire, I think. Better than a muddy puddle or a rotten apple on the ground, right?

But there are other times when I'd rather blend in. There are days I feel like this bold, brown stain in the middle of this big white canvas. Like one day, this boy who follows me and my friends around sometimes, asked a really dumb question. We were going on a field trip to the zoo, and my friend Mackenzie and I were at my locker putting on sunscreen. This idiot boy, Kevin, comes right up to me and says, "What are you putting sunscreen on for? You can't get burned!" Like just because I'm black I can't have sensitive skin and I can just run around in this thin air and bright sun with no protection? What a moron. I took a deep breath and told him that direct sunlight does kill brain cells, and he didn't have any to lose, so maybe he should find a hat. He didn't get it. Sometimes it's little things like that that get to me. And sometimes it's bigger stuff.

People can make really stupid assumptions sometimes. I hear boys in the hall, black and white, calling each other nasty racial names. A girl in my neighborhood just the other week asked how we could afford to live in such a nice house. I told her my mom is a lawyer and my dad is a CPA. I didn't mention that they're both white. I don't think that any of this is any of her business. But then I got to thinking, I am the only black person on our block, maybe even on our street. That's the bigger stuff, and that *does* bother me.

And then there's stuff I see on TV or hear on the news in the car in the morning. There's been this situation in a town down in Louisiana. That's the state where the hurricane hit so hard a few years ago, in case you don't know. This story isn't new, either, but people are still talking about it, so it must be pretty important. These black boys were put on trial for attempted murder for getting into a pretty bad fight with a white boy. All this happened at a school where some white kids had just hung nooses from a tree when black kids tried to sit there. Those white kids hardly got into any trouble. My mom and dad think I'm not paying attention, or I'm too young to be bothered too much about this. But I am *scared*. How can people still be treating each other like that today in the United Sates? It sounds like the way my parents have described South Africa to me, and I think there's something wrong with that picture.

But there's definitely good stuff too, and I told you I would tell you about all of that. I get to go to school here, and I'm learning *a lot*. I read all the time, especially history stories about girls. You'd be glad to know that I think I can do pretty much anything when I grow up. I'm not too good at spelling, but I try really hard. I want to be a doctor and help people who are sick like you, maybe even way over there.

Girls get treated about the same as boys around here. There's even a girl on the wrestling team at my school! Sometimes, though, I'm actually kind of glad that I don't have blonde hair and blue eyes. It's almost like there's this idea of what a girl here should look like, and some of my friends spend way too much time obsessing about that. Me, I'm never going to get there, so I just don't trouble myself with the thought of looking like a Barbie doll.

There are really a lot of things about my life that feel pretty good.

When I'm sick, I stay home snuggled under a bunch of blankets and my mom and dad get me medicine to make me better, no problem. Everyone gets to go to school if they want to, and everyone can make it through if they try. We have a two-story house with nine rooms. I have my own bedroom painted yellow with green flowers in a border against the ceiling. I have tons of clothes, nothing fancy, but enough so I can wear something new every day for a couple of weeks. I am never hungry. There is always food to eat in the fridge. Mom and Dad *love me.* They do. They about suffocate me with their hugs, and they tell me every day that I'm a supergirl.

So with all this, is it weird that I miss you, and I sometimes wonder what South Africa is like? I know that Soweto is a part of a city called Johannesberg, and it's a place where the black people lived separately for a long time so the white people wouldn't have to see them. I know that crime is very high there, especially against women. I know that there are a lot of orphans who have nobody to take care of them. All this makes me sad, but it also makes me mad. If this is the place you came from there must be some good. You kept me safe in your belly even though you knew you would have to raise me on your own. You worked even when you were sick and pregnant, and my parents say you never complained. You always had a smile on your face. I hope that I can be as strong as that some day.

I wish that I could meet you. I'd like to hold your hand, touch your face, and hold you tight. I'd like to sing you a song. Not to brag, but people think I have a beautiful voice. Maybe I got that from you. I'd like to thank you for giving me a chance, and for believing that I would make out better in a different place. I am doing fine because you let me go.

My friend Maggie carries a rabbit's foot for good luck. (I don't like to think about what happened to the rest of the rabbit.) She says it's her amulet to keep bad things from coming her way. I think that's not such a bad idea with so many wackos running loose and catastrophes going on in this crazy world.

In my mind's eye, I've painted a picture of you with long, shiny braids and the face of a queen, just like me. I carry you like an invisible amulet. You keep me safe. You remind me to think before I speak and look before I leap. You whisper in my ear late at night in your honey voice when I'm sad. You tell me it's ok to be afraid. I can almost, almost feel you in the room sometimes, sense the softest touch on my cheek. And I can't help wondering if maybe I was your amulet, too, in your dark moments. I hope so. I really do.

I love you Mama.

Naledi Miriam Murphy

FIGURATIVE LANGUAGE

I am like a mirage
My English teacher wants me
to write a simile
comparing two unlike things
using "like" or "as"
to describe myself
so a mirage is what I am
who I am
silver lines of
mystery shimmering
in a desert
I appear when you think you need me most
when you feel out of control
lost and afraid
you use me to claim your power again
to feel strong
then I disappear without a trace

And maybe you wonder where I've gone
but not for long
you just turn in a different direction
looking for a new resource
a different lifeline
maybe that's what it's like
to be me

You don't even know I'm here
most of the time
you're not aware that I exist
(sometimes I don't believe it myself)
because when I walk down these halls
I am invisible
solo

I try so hard to melt into the walls
to keep silent in the
flood of voices
if you do hear me
you turn to your friends and whisper
and laugh
and maybe it's not on purpose
but still
you move to the other side of the corridor
cross that imaginary border
(the one without a fence or a wall)
and look away

This is how I shimmer and glide
in the heat of discomfort
I fade
I choose to disintegrate
but you never try to stop me
maybe your eyes deceived you
just a trick of the light
And if I stand my ground
speak two languages fluently
(can you do that?)
throw my hair back
in a dark, triumphant wave
look you in the eye
and shyly smile
will you believe in me?

If I brush your arm as I pass by
just a whisper of contact
will you accept that
I am real
or will you run?

I hear you when you mutter
"Go Back to Mexico"
what if I told you
I've never even been?
that my Daddy brought my Mama here
five years before I was born?
Mexico is a mirage to me
Isn't that ironic?
(I'm listening in class
whether you choose
to believe me or not)

So what if
I won't surrender to the heat,
won't shiver and die
when the light changes
what if I keep the language
of my family
what if I dream
of desert sand across the border
because there people might see me --
no need for an optical illusion

and I guess this isn't really a simile
it's not comparing two unlike things
using a form of "like" or "as"
but maybe that isn't the point
after all
maybe what I need you to hear is
maybe what I need to believe for myself is
maybe what I need to say out loud is
that I am not a simile
closer to a metaphor
(but not quite) because
in the end
I am real

Lengua Figurativa

Yo soy como un espejismo
Mi maestra de ingles quiere que
escriba un símil
comparando dos cosas diferentes
usando "como" o "tan"
para describirme
entonces un espejismo es lo que soy
quien soy
líneas de plata de
misterio brillando
en un desierto
aparezco cuando crees que me necesitas mas
cuando te sientes sin control
perdido y con miedo
me usas para reclamar tú poder otra vez
y sentir de fuerte
luego desaparezco sin dejar huella

Y quizás te preguntas a donde fui
pero no por mucho tiempo
sólo te das la vuelta en otra dirección
buscando un nuevo recurso
una línea de vida diferente
quizás eso es lo que es ser yo

Tú ni siquiera sabes que estoy aquí
la mayoría del tiempo
no estás consciente que existo
(a veces no creo en mí misma)
porque cuando camino por estos pasillos
soy invisible
solo
trato con codas mis fuerzas a fundirme en   las paredes

mantener silencio en el
flujo de las voces
si tu me oyes
ves a tus amigos y susurras
y ríes
y quizás no es a propósito
pero de todos modos
te mueves al otro lado del pasillo
y cruzas esa frontera imaginaria
(esa sin una cerca o pared)
y apartas la vista

Eso es cómo brillo y me deslizo
en el calor de la incomodidad
me desaparece
opto por desintegrarme
pero nunca tratas de pararme
quizás te engañan tus ojos
sólo un truco de la luz

¿Y si me mantengo firme
hablo dos lenguas con fluidez
(puedes hacer eso?)
pongo mi pelo atrás
en un oscura, triunfante ola
te miro en el ojo y sonrío con timidez
me creerías?

¿Si rozo tu brazo
cuando te paso
sólo un susurro de contacto
aceptarías que
soy verdadera
o correrías?

Te oigo cuando musitas

"Regresa a México"
¿qué pasa si te digo
que aun nunca he estado?
¿que mí Papá trajó a mí Mamá aquí
cinco años antes de que naciera?
México es un espejismo para mi
¿No es irónico?
(estoy escuchando en la clase
si tú optas
por creerme o no)

¡Y qué? si
no me entrego al calor
no tiemblo y muerto
cuando cambia la luz
qué si mantengo el lenguaje
de mí familia
qué si sueño
con arena de desierto al otro lado de la frontera
porque allá la gente quizá pueda verme
no hay la necesidad para una ilusión óptica

y supongo que no es un símil verdadero
no está comparando dos cosas diferentes
usando un tipo de "como" o "tan"
pero quizás ese no es el punto
después de todo
quizás lo que necesito que oigas
quizás es lo que necesito creer por mí misma es
quizás lo que necesito decir en voz alta es
que no soy un símil
cercana a una metáfora
(pero no del todo) porque
al fin
yo soy verdadera

Atmospheric Aberrations and the Potential Effects of Global Climate Change on Predatorial Relationships in Human Adolescents

Or

THUNDER SNOW

I woke up last night to the most uncanny situation. Granted, the weather here is bizarre most of the time. In fact, there's a saying that if you don't appreciate the current weather in Colorado, just wait a minute. But this was beyond your run of the mill "blizzard in July" episode. When I attained verticality in my bed and looked out my window, lo and behold, there was thunder snow.

It was really extraordinary, peculiar and entrancing at the same time, mellifluous and treacherous. In the sodium glow of the streetlight on the corner I could see that it was snowing *exceptionally* hard. The ground harbored too much residual warmth for it to stick; the weather had actually been unseasonably hot for March for the past few weeks, but it was coming down! So what? Let me elaborate. This was not a solo performance from a solitary discombobulated snow cloud. This was a symphony, and the musicians sounded incensed. The wind was so strong that the snow flurries were actually blustering horizontally. And every few seconds the sky was illuminated an eerie, shadowy indigo, like the pall of a lightless room when you leave the TV on late into the night. Sheet lightning. Wicked strange. For the grand finale, there was *Big Thunder*. The variety that surrounds the house and makes the walls tremble, but all rumble-some and low. The kind that makes you momentarily vacate your skin even in the daylight. In the dark, it honestly sounded like the end of the world.

I was fully cognizant by this time, but no one else in the house appeared to be. I've been fairly edgy for the last few months and it's hard to settle when something is perturbing me. So I curled up into a fetal position under my covers and waited for the storm to abate. That's essentially the way my life proceeds at present, you see. I just sit silent and still and hope that no one will detect me, that the negative energy will dissipate like rain on an August pavement.

After a time, my room refrained from its cabaret of demented silhouettes. The windows stopped clattering, and the blizzard suddenly seemed to rage away to Kansas powered by that outlandish wind. If only the storm would end like that at school tomorrow. But I knew that it was more complicated than the weather outside. The difficulties at school were violent and tempestuous, but they weren't going anywhere in the foreseeable future.

When I can't drop off, which is the majority of nights, my brain activates and remains in high gear until I essentially pass out from exhaustion. According to my cell, the storm concluded at about 2:11 a.m.

Lying there for the next few hours I considered how much I dreaded the next day, not for any particular reason. I dread every day. Any time I can accomplish it, I create an imaginative illness so I can remain at home. This isn't because I don't enjoy the academic nature of school; if you hadn't already guessed by my wacky word choice, I actually relish the acquisition of fresh knowledge. I despise the institution because of the people involved. Lying in bed I contemplated Sean Franklin and Heather Trevinsky and Lisa Cook. I pondered the root causes of my anger and fear. I thought about the possibility that no one loved me and no one understood me. I toyed with the dark, unspeakable prospect of being able to sleep on and on and not wake up. It went something like this.

2:48 a.m. I recall the beginning of the school year. Being a 7th grade girl is unpleasant regardless of who you are, I believe. Even the trendy, popular girls seem to devote much of their time to worrying about whether they're wearing the "right" clothes, about which boys they're trying to impress... not so much time bothering about homework, and no time wondering how other people feel.

But I'm not pretty, or well-liked. I know I don't sport the "right" clothes, but in order to do this, several cosmic factors need to align. You have to have some money, you have to know where to find the "right" clothes, and I'm fairly sure you have to have a parent who will transport you and help you pick them out. I'm doomed in all three areas.

So what do I have on my side? Not much. I'm not obese, but I'm not anorexic, either. I'm quite tall, and a bit shapeless, lacking curves, if you can envision that. I choose a lot of brown and grey baggy clothes. They conceal my body to the greatest degree possible. No one's ever enlightened me on the subject of how to make colors complement each other or how to assemble a stunning ensemble. Sometimes I'm actually jealous of the way certain girls look like they've just stepped out of a magazine, so entirely put together. I don't understand that phenomenon at all. On the one hand, I'm somewhat interested, but I'm far too shy to ask. On the other hand, in a variety of ways, I want to be nothing like any of them.

My hair is a dilemma. It is absolutely, nastily straight as a board, and it's lanky. Even though I shower religiously every morning, by the end of the day my locks look greasy. I know people assume I don't have proper hygiene, and it humiliates me. But a large proportion of my problem is that I am hopelessly shy. I can't ask anyone for help with any of these issues. We moved here over the summer, and I still don't know really anyone. I'm too terrified of being ridiculed, or being ignored. I know everyone at school despises me.

Most days so far this year I have commenced sobbing as soon as I have gotten home and been able to slink up into my room. Breaking down in front of my mom (my dad's usually not home yet) has no positive effect. She just threatens to enroll me in a private school, as if that would make any difference. So I remain upstairs and wait for a miracle to occur.

3:19 a.m. My brain has decided to torture me with how the teasing began on the first day of 7ᵗʰ grade. I boarded the bus silently in the hopes that my attempt at being inconspicuous would be rewarded with pity. It was exceptionally crowded. Mine was the final stop before the ten-minute ride to school. That day, ten minutes morphed into an eternity for me. All the seats were already filled with two, or crammed with three people. I found the closest bench occupied by a pair of girls who appeared fairly harmless. That was my initial mistake. Appearances can be deceiving. Lisa Cook became my first middle school tormentor.

She and her friend spent those ten minutes cackling maniacally as they attempted to push me off the seat and on to the gummy floor. When Lisa observed that I didn't have pierced ears, she retrieved a mechanical pencil from her backpack and began to jab at my lobes with it. I didn't want to make a fuss. I didn't want to get in trouble with the bus driver. I also didn't want anyone else to notice me, so I focused all my attention on clenching all the muscles in my legs and my derriere so I didn't topple out of the seat. By the time the "ride" terminated at the school, my thighs were on fire from the exertion.

From that day forward Lisa made a point of informing as many people as possible on that bus to banish me from their seats. My best guess is that a lot of the kids didn't even know her, and they certainly didn't know me. It just seemed like a hilarious game with a delectable target. No big deal, right? Is that what you think? It was only a short ride. But to me, it was like surgery with no anesthesia. How would you feel if you walked into a crowded room and found that most of the people in there were planning to humiliate you? To torment you? To make you as uncomfortable as possible? Welcome to my world.

So why didn't I tell anyone? I did. My mom insisted that the kids would stop, that if she called the school it would probably just get worse. She suggested that bullies generally get bored and move on to someone else. Surprised at my own pluck, I finally went to the school office by myself and inquired about other busses. I discovered that there was one a mile up the hill from my house that I could ride. So without asking my parents, I made a decision. I had no arsenal of techniques to staunch the abuse, so I chose escape.

3:43 a.m. I'm remembering the longest walk. On a Monday morning in October I started getting up a half hour early to trudge up Calypso Drive. Things were acceptable for a time. Two girls, Heather Trevinsky and Jenny Underhill, would chat with me at the bus stop. They just seemed curious because I was "new." I started to trust them. I even laughed sometimes at their inane jokes. They belonged to a group of girls who were essentially obsessed with horses and riding. I knew nothing about these topics, but it was good not to be the center of attention for a change, so I remained in the shadows, listening, staying out of harm's way.

But then things deteriorated. I was out sick for a week with an evil case of the flu. I returned to the bus stop on a Tuesday morning. Still feeling rather shaky, I made my way to the top of the hill. Once I got there, I knew, too late, that I should have stayed in bed. Without fair warning, my stomach lurched. I reached the scrub oaks lining the sidewalk before retching my guts out. I staggered back home, regurgitating time after time on the way. In the distance I heard voices giggling back at the bus stop and shrieking, "Nasty!" and "Can you believe she just did that? What a loser!" Naturally, the voices were my "friends," Jenny and Heather. I just didn't understand. It's not like I threw up on purpose. I was actually ill. How could I possibly deserve to be teased for that? But there was no logic to the abuse; I suppose the predator doesn't have to justify the stalking of its prey in most situations.

Then the texting and emailing began. Heather and Jenny seriously must have devoted an hour every night for the next couple of weeks composing horrible things to say about me, not even anything to do with the whole vomit extravaganza. It's as though they had been waiting their whole lives for a victim, for someone less socially acceptable than them, and I appeared and made their dream come true. I stopped checking my mail, stopped answering my phone.

There wasn't another alternate bus, and I did tell my parents. Every time I received a new message and dissolved into tears, my mom told me to just ignore it. Finally, when the jokes turned to threats about "showing up at their bus stop," my mom contacted the school. The girls were reprimanded, told how inappropriate they were, and to leave me alone. The result? They informed every one of their friends that I had "ratted them out." The dynamic duo became an army of a dozen overnight. I couldn't walk down the halls at school without getting attacked by snide whispers and giggles. It was like a black, oily tide rushing over me, and I was surely drowning.

But unbelievably, the worst was yet to come. Once you become the one who is bullied, it's like you're wearing a t-shirt announcing your status. Everyone who needs a whipping boy is drawn to you like an irresistible magnet. You're the center of that freakish storm, and the thunder and wind and snow and lightning are all focusing in on you, pummeling you, trying to see how long it will take for you to break.

4:32 a.m. The ultimate monster has forced its way into my brain. Sean Franklin, I believe, has a finely-tuned bully radar. He can sense innately when someone is injured, when they don't have any support, when they feel trapped, and he moves in for the kill. He is tall, gangly, and blonde. He forever has dirt under his fingernails, and he chews on them almost as much as I chew on mine, though I can't imagine what he has to worry about. He is at the top of the middle school food chain. You can fill in the blanks to figure out where I fit into that cycle. Sean is simply dangerous-looking. He confidently struts down the hall, ramming people out of his way, ogling girls he likes and commenting shamelessly on their bodies, and watching out for people like me. His eyes dart from side to side like a snake scoping out its next meal. When he first saw me skirting the 7th grade hallway one Monday morning, head ducked, books clutched to my chest, he decided it was time for a feast.

Sean was in my homeroom. In that drafty, musty-smelling portable I spent my twenty-five minutes a day quietly observing other people, trying to meld into the walls. I could name you everyone in my class, describe their clothes, the kind of gum they chewed, because I watch and I try to remember. It's a survival technique, I suppose. My homeroom teacher was Ms. Mortenson. She was a P.E. teacher, and didn't seem terribly interested in whether or not we actually did homework. She required the room to be silent. Most days she read the paper with her tennis shoes propped on top of the desk, blocking her line of vision for the classroom.

Notes don't make much noise. From the first day that Sean Franklin noticed me, a crumpled up wad of paper was left on my desk at the beginning of every homeroom period, dropped casually by his grimy hands. He made no attempt to hide the fact that he was delivering these missives. In fact, he usually stood next to my desk with a savage grin on his face for a few seconds after each deposit, assessing the damage he had inflicted.

The notes ranged from roughly sketched pictures of parts of the male body I barely even recognized, to chicken-scratched, badly spelled phrases about how ugly I was, to lists of animals that he thought smelled worse than me. Sometimes he would just write a single curse word or a picture of a gun or a knife dripping blood, or a list of words like "hate," "monster," and "dirty"…you get the idea. For the first time I really moved past humiliation and shame to fear. I was terrified that he was going to follow me somewhere and hurt me, and I didn't even know why. I only knew that I was a non-person in this school, that no one would notice if Sean Franklin killed me and left me in a dark corner. I had no value to this particular community.

I told the teacher. I even gave her some of the notes. She said that Sean was just playing; she suggested that he "liked" me. How moronic is that? She said she would change his seat. It's so absurd to me that a grown up can be so afraid of a kid, a twelve year old, that it makes them blind. Or maybe she simply didn't care. Either way, it didn't help me one bit. This was the most fun Sean had had all year, and a new desk wasn't going to deter him.

Maybe it's because it was a boy (like the girls weren't dangerous?) this time, but when I told my mom what was happening, she finally told Mr. Kwan, the counselor, everything that had happened so far that year. She expounded significantly about someone needing to stand up for her poor little girl at that school. We had just learned about irony in my LA class. What a perfect example.

Mr. Kwan changed my schedule. He found me some "nice" girls, girls who looked as scared and lonely as me, to sit with at lunch. So we all started to huddle there together over our sack lunches, not talking, not making eye contact, barely eating. But psychically, we all knew the truth. We were the unwanted, the despised, the defective. That is what we had in common, and what we knew with certainty. People fanned out widely around our table as though we had some contagious disease. They still laughed and sometimes pointed, but there really is safety in numbers, I think. We sat together and knew that we all felt much the same way. We would all rather be stranded forever on a desert island than be noticed in that cafeteria.

A further irony is that assimilation could be my salvation. I want someone to educate me in the fine art of camouflage, on how to morph into a giggling, goofy, twit of a girl, dressed like a photocopy of all the rest, who manages to do something creative with her hair every morning. I need someone to teach me how to make a friend who won't break my heart; how to respond to someone speaking to me, even someone friendly, without tears welling up in my eyes; how to navigate a hallway with my head up, without my legs cramping and my heart racing, with palms that don't perspire. I don't think these are difficult tasks really, but they are tasks you have to be taught. And instead of helping me learn, people turn their heads away like I'm a freak in a circus side show.

Perhaps you're thinking it's not as bad as all that. I'm surely overreacting to all of this. But what if this was your life every day? What if your limbs ached every night because you'd remained so tense all day long? And then, even though you were desperate to sleep, you couldn't, because the images of your day kept pummeling your brain like thunder snow, pretending to be harmless and promising to melt away, but then creeping up behind you to scream at you, to remind you that you're never safe, not really. Not in the end. But like I said, thunder snow is temporary. My life has been this frenetic storm for months now. I am ripe for a drastic meteorological turn of events.

I am not like those kids at Columbine, or the shooters I frequently hear about on public radio in the morning. I do not resemble them, nor do I pity them. I will not take my anger and my fear out on innocent people. But some day, it would be really fabulous if someone would notice that I am innocent too. I don't hurt or laugh at people. When I try to work out what I've done to offend so much, it seems like just my being alive is a problem.

5:48 a.m. I am exhausted, but I have to start planning how I'm going to face this day at school. What if Casie Peterson is the answer? Could it actually be true? Yesterday, one of the girls at the lepers' lunch table walked in with Casie. She is short with long blond hair. She has a mouthful of braces that you can see really clearly, because Casie smiles all the time. Her personality bubbles out of her, like a slightly demented water feature with fiber-optic illumination. She chatters constantly even if no one is actually listening. Everyone at the table witnessed her grand entrance in a kind of awe.

Casie's just a sort of "regular" looking girl I suppose, but I think she's stunning. She came over to the table and didn't laugh and stare. She talked to all the rejects like we were human beings, and to top it all off, she sat down. She didn't even stop talking as she threw her leg over the bench and squeezed herself in, right next to me. Somewhere in her babble about her band teacher, she asked for one of my carrot sticks, and went ahead and acquired one before I had time to answer. Not that I could find a voice to reply. I was completely shocked. I wanted to offer her my whole lunch, to move out of the way so she could have the whole bench to herself. And more than that, I really wanted to cry. Casie didn't care who she was sitting with, and for that I think she is the most courageous and charismatic person in the world. If I have to amend my persona in order to achieve anonymity, this is who I want to be. Casie Peterson. Perhaps she could show me how.

And for the first time in months I saw a sliver of natural light in the clouds. For a few minutes, until Casie, still speaking, rose and wandered off to another table, the thunder in my head paused. The darkness lifted, almost imperceptibly. Maybe not everyone automatically despised me. Maybe I had a chance to survive this nightmare.

6:30 a.m. My alarm shrills, as if I need something to wake me. I haven't slept since the beginning of the storm. I start to hear the others stirring, water running in my parents' bathroom. Led Zeppelin suddenly blares from my brother's room. They have no idea that I have been awake all this time, planning my survival strategy like a contestant on some twisted reality show. But I have to get up now, I suppose. The sun is up and there are literally *no* clouds in the sky. Icy blue, no sign of what occurred a few hours ago. I'm the only one in the house who knows. It was my private tempest. But maybe somebody out there witnessed it, just from a different vantage point. It's difficult to say what complications or revelations this new day will present, but I'll tackle them just the same. I don't believe I really have a choice, in the end.

MARGIN NOTES

The following is a *Tiger Talk* exclusive, *Tiger Talk* being the name of our awesome student newspaper here at Trenton Middle School. One talented reporter (me) was assigned to interview five students new to our gigantic building with the hopes of welcoming them into the school community. I'm not sure what that means, but Mr. Samson told me to do it. So do it I did. Wow, that was a bad sentence for a budding journalist. I chose a student who moved here from New Jersey, an 8th grader who plays sax in the jazz band, a superstar basketball player, a 6th grade boy who had *a lot* of trouble talking through his braces, and Elizabeth.

Elizabeth caught my attention the moment she walked in the door. She is tall; she towers over most of the boys, even though she's in 7th grade. Her hair, the day I talked to her, was dyed pitch black with hot pink streaks. Her clothes, you might guess, were all black: skinny black jeans, Jack Skellington t-shirt, black hoodie. Elizabeth's face stood out because of the, you guessed it, black eyeliner drawn thickly all the way around her eyes. (This actually made her eyes stand out... they are this amazing deep, blue color like the ocean right after the sun goes down.) The day we spoke she was wearing purple lipstick so dark it looked black until I saw her up close. Elizabeth wears 23 (I counted) bracelets, black and silver, over both arms, and has her ears pierced three times on the left side and four times on the right. Her fingernails were painted black, but bitten down so close to her fingers that they were chipped and cracked. Elizabeth looks a little like a ghost to me, and that's why I picked her. She kind of glides through the halls like a human whisper in Vans. I wondered about her, and I heard kids talk about her behind her back, so being a responsible reporter, I went in search of answers.

Ben:	So Elizabeth, tell me about yourself. Where are you from? How did you end up here?
Elizabeth:	Ummmm…Can we talk about something else? That's really boring stuff.
Ben:	Uh…ok. Why not?
Elizabeth:	No drama, all right? We just moved, so I started coming here. It's close to our condo.
Ben:	Ok, ok, no need to bite my head off. Just curious! We'll move on to another question, and if you feel like revealing the deep, dark secrets of your past later on, we'll come back to them.
Elizabeth:	Not likely, no deep, dark secrets here. Can we just get this over with please?
Ben:	With pleasure. So Elizabeth, why do you dress the way you do? Attention? Color blindness?
Elizabeth:	Wow, you're obnoxious. You know that, right? You're lucky I'm even talking to you. Why do you dress the way *you* do?
Ben:	Well, because I'm just a normal person.
Elizabeth:	So I'm not normal?
Ben:	Who's asking the questions here?
Elizabeth:	Gee, I'm sorry. They're such excellent questions. You are a real moron, you know that?
Ben:	OK, this isn't going exactly the way I had planned. Maybe we should just cut this short. If you want to be unfriendly and…well…weird, feel free. I think we're done here.
Elizabeth:	Seriously? That's all you can take? A little pressure and you run away with your tail between your legs? How would you like it if everyone judged you right away because of the way you dressed? Try thinking before

	you speak.
Ben:	I am thinking…about shutting off the microphone.
Elizabeth:	*(Heavy sigh)* I dress the way I do because it's part of who I am. Black and white and red are vivid, everyone notices you when you walk in a room, but at the same time they go together. I like these colors. I'm kind of a dark, quiet person, if you haven't already figured that out. My clothes make a statement, they make me stand out, but they scare most people too. So I get to be myself, but people usually leave me alone, too. *Most* people…
Ben:	So who are your role models? Marilyn Manson? Kurt Cobain?
Elizabeth:	Awesome assumption you're making there. Marilyn Manson is a totally artificial loser who puts on a show and hopes he'll get paid for it. Kurt Cobain wasted his life. Total genius, threw it away.
Ben:	Ok, then, break the stereotype. Answer the question!
Elizabeth:	Louis Armstrong, and my mom.
Ben:	Huh?
Elizabeth:	You are *really* eloquent aren't you? My mom is the strongest person ever. She lets me be who I am without judging me, and she is kind to everyone, even if they've treated her like dirt. You can't say that about many people. She's super-smart, too.
Ben:	Fair enough, but Louis Armstrong? Musician, right?
Elizabeth:	Duh.
Ben:	I'll pretend I didn't hear that comment.
Elizabeth:	Then I'll repeat it for you. Duh. Louis Armstrong was a musical god. He wrote the simplest songs in the world, but they wind themselves around your guts and your brain and your heart and squeeze until the emotion he's getting at oozes out of you like you made the music yourself. Here. Listen to this.
	(We pause the interview as I put on her mp3 player and listen to something called, "It's a Wonderful World.")
Ben:	That was really pretty, but I don't get it. It's just a happy song. You don't strike me as too happy.

Elizabeth:	So because of the way I look I'm supposed to go home and hurt myself or something? I'm pretty content with my life, actually, and I bet I spend a whole lot less time worrying about what people think of me than you do. Did you actually even listen to the song? He's not just talking about the pretty flowers and birdies, you dork. He's talking about balance. For every sunny day there's a cloudy one, the nighttime is as beautiful and important as the day, and it's all good. Because you can't have one side without the other and expect there to be anything wonderful about your world. Open your ears. Seriously.
Ben:	Ummm…maybe I should listen to it again.
	(We pause again. I close my eyes and listen. The song ends quietly, and I literally jump out of my seat when the next song blasts into my brain.)
Ben:	What happened to Louis Armstrong? What is this?
Elizabeth:	You're yelling. And it's Nine Inch Nails. Like I said, it's all about balance.
Ben:	Maybe we should move on. So Elizabeth, what do you want to be when you get out of school?
Elizabeth:	Are you trying to sound like a game show host? You're doing a really good job. Do we get to do a bonus round next?
Ben:	Just answer the question, please?
Elizabeth:	A scientist. I want to help cure diseases that are killing kids in countries that our government likes to ignore. Every child matters. What? Were you expecting me to say self-obsessed computer geek? Hairdresser? Hermit?
Ben:	What's a hermit?
Elizabeth:	What's a cretin?
Ben:	Now you're just being mean.
Elizabeth:	Maybe you should send someone competent to do your job next time. I'm going to change the world, dude. I don't go home and crawl under a blanket and cry, you know. Check out the Heifer Project, or ONE or Free Rice. If kids like us don't make a change to fix the mess

	out parents have made, who will? Kids are *dying*. That's not ok with me. Is it ok with you?
Ben:	I guess not. I guess it's not something I've ever really thought about.
Elizabeth:	Maybe you should.
Ben:	Maybe I will.
Elizabeth:	Good.
Ben:	Fine.
Elizabeth:	Next question?
Ben:	Ummm…so how *do* you respond when kids make comments about you?
Elizabeth:	You mean kids like you? Don't bother answering that. I know kids talk about me. That's all right. I saw a bumper sticker the other day that said "The More You Disapprove, The More Fun It Is For Me." That's pretty much the way I feel. I stand out because I don't *want* to look like everyone else. I don't want you to think that I'll be who you want me to be. If that makes people talk, whatever. I'm used to it. I get that stuff all the time, wherever I go. Case closed.
Ben:	I thought we were finally getting somewhere.
Elizabeth:	Ummm..you don't seem to have any idea where you are going. How could you possibly be getting somewhere? So I just kind of blow it off here when people are talking about me when I pass by. I don't like it, who would? But I know people don't really know who I am and it's mostly because of the way I look. And it's my choice to dress this way, and I like it, so I deal.
Ben:	Well, it sounds like you're kind of tough, so what is the hardest thing about being in this school?
Elizabeth:	Well, there's a lot of pressure here. I mean, to be the "normal" kid like you were saying. But I can ignore that. The hardest thing, I guess, is that in the three weeks I've been here, except for teachers and partners on stuff in class, you're the first person who has talked to me. And you're only doing it for an assignment. I don't bite, you know. I'm not some freak of nature or a vampire

	or something. I'm just a kid. And it gets kind of lonely being who you are all the time with no one to talk to.
Ben:	So if you're wanting some friends, why don't you talk to people?
Elizabeth:	In case you haven't noticed, people run in packs here. Most of these kids have known each other since kindergarten. It's kind of hard to push your way in when the Alpha is saying no way.
Ben:	So you haven't made any friends here?
Elizabeth:	Not unless I include you. But I'm thinking about maybe showing up for one of the meetings of your newspaper club. I'm a pretty good photographer. That's kind of why I agreed to do this interview.
Ben:	Oh. That's cool. Mr. Samson's always looking for new blood.
Elizabeth:	Great choice of words.
Ben:	Sorry. So what is your favorite subject and why?
Elizabeth:	I like to write. I write all the time in a journal, and I have my own blog. I write poems and put them on my page all the time. So my favorite part is my L.A. class when we get to write about what we want.
Ben:	What are your poems usually about?
Elizabeth:	I write a lot about the way I'm feeling. That's the way I deal with knowing that I don't fit in so well. Sometimes I write reviews of books I've read or songs I've downloaded, too. If I'm mad about something that's going on in the world I write letters. I don't ever send them, but I write them anyways.
Ben:	Geez. I never met anyone before who wrote for anything other than school. That's kind of cool in a weird sort of way.
Elizabeth:	Thanks, I think.
Ben:	Ok, what is one thing you would like people to know about you?
Elizabeth:	Haven't you figured that out by now?
Ben:	Well…do you want me to guess?
Elizabeth:	No, I want you to listen.

Ben:	I *have* been listening! I've been taking notes!
Elizabeth:	Then you'd know already. You'd know what I want people to know. There's nothing else I can tell you. My work here is done.
Ben:	So I basically just wasted a half hour of my life?
Elizabeth:	If you say so.
Ben:	And because you're stubborn, and mean, and....and crazy, I'm suppose to be psychic? Whatever.
Elizabeth:	Your social skills really bite, you know that? What I want you to know is that I *am* different, and that's a *good* thing. Wouldn't it be great if we could all look at what's weird about each other and say, "Oooohhh! I wish I could be like that," instead of "Eeeewwwwww! How freaky is that?" I want people to know that I'm good with who I am. I'm not depressed, I don't hate you, I don't hate myself. I don't sit in the dark every waking hour, or obsess about death all the time. I actually like to go for long walks in the sun. I like the color green. I sometimes read goofy romance books and watch stupid cartoons. I like to eat dinner at the dining room table with my family and play with my dog. It's that balance thing again. Capice?
Ben:	Ka-what?
Elizabeth:	I give. This is a lost cause.
Ben:	No it's not. I got a great interview!
Elizabeth:	But do you know who I am?
Ben:	Sure! You're Elizabeth. Duh.
Elizabeth:	Well, that's a start I guess.
Ben:	So do you want to come and meet Mr. Samson?
Elizabeth:	I guess it wouldn't hurt. He has to be more interesting than you.
Ben:	That's it. I'm turning off the microphone.
Elizabeth:	The truth hurts sometimes, Ben. Learn to accept it while you're young.

And so ends my exposé of the dark side of student life here at Trenton Middle. The funny thing is, Elizabeth turned out to be sort of the opposite of dark in a lot of ways, not what I was expecting at all. Who knows? Maybe next month I'll write a biographical piece about Louis Armstrong. It turns out that peeking outside my comfort zone is actually kind of fun. Maybe Elizabeth will collaborate with me. Stranger things have happened, occasionally.

Notes on Margin Notes

*This is going to sound like an acceptance speech, so stop reading now if you're expecting something profound! Thank you to Arghavan for an objective reading of "Skyscrapers." Thanks to Megan for the editorial support and the calm objectivity. Thank you to Jas for reading and re-reading my drafts more times than he cares to remember, even after Rowan threw up on them on the way back from Taos. Thank you to Alison for the meticulous and beautiful translation of "Figurative Language." Thank you to my parents for always knowing that I was a writer. Thank you to Sheila for helping me to survive middle school. Thank you to the life-altering Colorado Writing Project without which I would not have had the time or confidence to begin this work in earnest. But most of all, than you to all of the students who have inspired me over the years. I am forever in awe of you for what you teach **me** every day.*

Printed in the United States
146597LV00004B/5/P